HIS
INVISIBLE
WIFE

HIS
INVISIBLE
WIFE

SHELIA M. GOSS

URBAN BOOKS

www.urbanbooks.net

URBAN SOUL is published by

Urban Books
1199 Straight Path
West Babylon, NY 11704

ISBN-13: 978-1-59983-085-8
ISBN-10: 1-59983-085-X

First Printing: July 2009
10 9 8 7 6 5 4 3 2 1

Printed in the United States of America

ACKNOWLEDGMENTS

Without God strengthening me when I was weak and sustaining me through this journey, I would be lost. There's not enough space in any book for me to share how thankful I am to God for all that He's done for me.

I'm grateful to have had two parents, Lloyd (1947–96) and Exie Goss, who showed me love and encouraged me to follow my dreams. I also have to thank my brothers, Lloyd (aka Jerry) and John, my cousin Dorothy Hodges, and the Hogan family (aunts, uncles, and cousins) for their support, with a special shout-out to Hattie and Nicolette—my unofficial street team.

A very special thanks to the people who made this book possible: my agent, Maxine Thompson; my publisher, Carl Weber, and the Urban Books team; and those working behind the scenes at Kensington Books.

I really appreciate all the readers, book clubs, bookstores, and librarians who have chosen my books. I can't thank you enough. Toni Templeton (Sisters Sippin' Tea), thank you for the standing invite to your book club's annual tea party in Longview, Texas. A special thanks to the ladies of the SistahFriend Book Club, Page Turners Book

Club, GirlFriends Inc. of Memphis, and Mindful Thinker's Book Club of Dallas; to Yasmin Coleman (APOOO Book Club) and MaShawn (SBS Book Club); to Kemmerly Beckham, Charlotte Blocker, and Brenda Evans in Dallas, Texas; to Kimber An in Alaska; and Janice Spence in the UK. Kandie Delley of KanDel Media, thanks for the banners. Thank you, Sharon "Shaye" Gray, for your honest feedback. To the people I've met on MySpace and in the Yahoo! Groups (especially Live, Love, Laugh and Books and Essentially Woman), thanks for the support. To Elisa Leary and Shantal Young, thank you for your feedback.

I want to thank the following authors for their support: Gwyneth Bolton, Carla Curtis, Bettye Griffin, Linda Grosvenor, Donna Hill, Paula Hyman, Monica Jackson, Peggy Eldridge-Love, Angelia Menchan, Cherlyn Michaels, Michelle McGriff, Michelle Monkou, Celeste O. Norfleet, Eric Pete, Cydney Rax, V. Anthony Rivers, and John Wooden. I know I'm forgetting someone, so I'll stop the list here.

If I forgot to mention anyone, it was not intentional. Charge it to my head and not my heart. I appreciate you all.

Shelia M. Goss

I

WHAT GOES AROUND COMES AROUND

CHAPTER 1

Sleepless nights fueled Brianna Mayfield's desire to avenge the hardships that had fallen upon her father. She had watched Robert Mayfield go from a strong and passionate man to one who barely had enough energy to get out of bed daily. To see him lose hope after being rejected several times for a business loan had torn her up inside. If only he would have received the loan from JB Savings and Loan, their neighborhood bank. It would have been enough for him to keep his store, Mayfield Groceries, open; without it, he hadn't been able to compete with the chain stores. Seeing all his dreams deteriorate in front of her eyes had left a bitter taste in Brianna's mouth.

Brianna fantasized about the day the guilty party would pay retribution. She vowed to make it slow and painful. She wanted to see Jack Banks, the owner of JB Savings and Loan, suffer the way she had watched her father suffer until his death. During her research, she had discovered that his nephew, Jacob Banks, had a thriving business, Banks Telecom, because of funding received from

JB Savings and Loan. Destroying Jacob's reputation in the business world would hurt his uncle, so Brianna had put her plan in motion and had gotten a job at Banks Telecom. When old man Banks died before she could fully implement her plan to destroy Jacob's company, she had decided to continue on her quest. Getting revenge on his favorite nephew would have to suffice.

Brianna prided herself on her work and usually excelled at whatever she did, whether it was maintaining her straight four-point-zero grade point average in graduate school or handling multimillion-dollar projects. Because of her father, she had majored in business and had become a certified public accountant after taking the exam only once. Her original plan had been to take over her father's store and expand it. Some of her coworkers at Banks Telecom accused her of being antisocial, but she wasn't there to make friends; she was there to get revenge, so she ignored their rants.

"Slow down," one of her coworkers said when Brianna accidentally bumped into two people as she rushed to catch the elevator.

"Got a meeting, and I can't be late," she responded while pushing her hand in between the elevator doors just before they closed.

Brianna pressed the button for the fourteenth floor and waited. Her mind went over what she would say. Normally, when she met with Jacob Banks, there were other people in the room. She hoped the anger festering in her system would subside long enough for her to make it through the one-on-one meeting with the CEO of Banks Telecom.

When her manager had informed her that she

had been summoned because of the fiasco with her last project, Brianna had scrambled to get her documentation together. Although she was guilty of setting up another employee by giving him inaccurate data, she refused to be the scapegoat for his mistake. As one of the lead accountants, Brianna had access to confidential company records and was regularly pulled in to work on various outside projects geared toward generating more money for the company.

She had used her position to hurt Jacob Banks internally and had done so without bringing much attention to herself. Brianna had a way of forging numbers and making things look better than what they were. Because of that, she knew it would only be a matter of time before Banks Telecom would face a financial crisis or she would be fired because someone was on to her. As she headed to this meeting with the CEO, she had a feeling she would know soon.

The elevator opened to a plush office filled with soft off-white carpet, and a petite, middle-aged woman sitting behind her desk immediately acknowledged her. "There you are. He's been asking for you," Joan Carlise stated as she escorted Brianna to Jacob's office.

Brianna glanced at her watch. According to it, she still had two minutes to spare. She sighed as the door to his office opened. Jacob stood up immediately and greeted her with a firm handshake. He was over six feet tall. He towered over her by at least five inches even though she wore heels.

"Thank you for coming at such short notice," he said as he motioned for her to sit down in the maroon leather chair.

She watched him walk back behind his long cherrywood desk as she took a seat and crossed her legs. The walls of his office were filled with small-business award plaques from various organizations. Up until the last quarter, Banks Telecom had been growing fast. Now the small company was facing a crisis.

"I know you're wondering why I called you here, so I won't take up too much of your time," he began.

Brianna remained quiet.

He tapped a pen on his desk. It annoyed her, but she tried to ignore it by focusing on his eyes. The twinkle in his gray eyes caused her to shift in her seat. She didn't have the cushion of having other people in the room. She was now face-to-face with Jacob Banks, all by herself. She rubbed her sweaty palms on her skirt.

"Brianna, you've been working for me for how long now?"

"For about a year," she responded.

"You trust me, don't you?"

Brianna looked away for a brief second before looking back into his eyes. "As much as the next man."

His eyebrows shifted. "I'll take that. How would you feel about a raise?"

Startled, because she was expecting a reprimand, she took a few seconds to respond. "I would welcome it with open arms."

"It's yours. I'll have my lawyers draw up the papers. After this year you can retire if you want, because I want to offer you a million-dollar raise."

Brianna looked around for the hidden cameras and then looked over the rim of her glasses. "Mr. Banks, you should have told me we were going to be on TV." She ran her hand through her shoulder-length, straight jet-black hair. "I would have done something else to my hair."

"First of all, call me Jacob. No, call me Jake. All I need for you to do is to agree to be my wife for a year, and the million dollars is yours."

At this point Brianna couldn't control herself. She burst out laughing, because she knew this was a practical joke. This couldn't be real. Here she was, thinking she had been caught forging numbers, and instead, he was offering her a million dollars. "This is ludicrous. As much as I'm flattered by this offer of a raise, why would I take you seriously?"

"I've been watching you for the last few months. You're intelligent, and you're beautiful. What man wouldn't want you by his side?"

"True." Brianna knew she was attractive to most men, but it still didn't answer the million-dollar question. "But the question is, why would you?"

Brianna was confused by the whole ordeal. What in the world would make him ask her, of all people? From what she had observed, he had his pick of women, and she was sure any one of them would love to be Mrs. Banks.

"We would be good together. I've seen you in meetings. You're not afraid to speak your mind. I find that an attractive quality, especially since I have enough yes-men around me."

She folded her arms and leaned back in her chair as Jake tried to plead his case.

"I looked over your personnel file, and it seems we're around the same age. We like some of the same things, from what I've gathered from our brief conversations over the past few months."

Brianna's mind was running a mile a minute.

She zoned out on him a few times as she tried to figure out his ulterior motive. She felt there was more to it than he was telling her, and she was determined to find out what it was. She interrupted him. "Let's cut through the bull. I need the *real* reason."

Jake blinked a few times. His beautiful eyes seemed to pierce her soul. Without blinking, he said, "My late uncle left me no choice."

Why would his uncle want him to marry her? Had he felt some remorse on his deathbed? The fact that Jack Banks had known how much pain he had caused her father made her stomach turn. The ache in Brianna's heart for her dad's last days threatened her sanity. She pushed those thoughts to the back of her mind.

This could be the opportunity she had been waiting for. Brianna would have access to millions as his wife. She didn't want to seem too eager, so she pretended to oppose the idea. "I don't mean to sound crude, but Mr. Banks, I mean Jake, you're a nice-looking man, and I'm sure you can find some other willing participant. I'm not available."

"If you're talking about your boyfriend, Charles. I took care of him already."

Brianna uncrossed her legs and sat straight up. "Excuse me?"

"He was more than happy to take the money he was offered and backed down. He'll be calling you later to get his stuff."

"How dare you interfere in my life like this!" she snapped. She didn't know if she was more furious at Jake or Charles, her boyfriend of the last year. If Brianna's brown-sugar complexion had been lighter, Jake would have been able to see how flushed her cheeks were.

The throbbing in her head intensified. First, his uncle had interfered in her father's life, and now Jake thought that because he had a little money, he could interfere in her personal life. She didn't know what to think about Charles. As soon as she got a hold of him, she would tell him a few choice words as well. She clenched her fists. Her nails dug into her palms to the point where she almost screamed.

Jake seemed confident and smug. "Maybe I went about this the wrong way. Let me explain."

She inched to the edge of her seat, and it took all her might not to reach across the desk and slap the smug look off Jake's face. She had to take control of the situation. Brianna stood up and didn't wait for Jake's explanation. She stormed out of the room. His secretary called out to her, but Brianna ignored her. The elevator wasn't coming fast enough, so she took the stairs. Her coworkers curiously eyed her as she stormed to her cubicle.

She blocked out the noise in the office and leaned back in her chair. She hated Jacob Banks more so now than ever. Up until this point, Brianna's revenge had been fueled by Jake's uncle's actions; now Jake had made it about his own actions. All she could think about was how Jake had manipulated his way into her personal life without any remorse. His uncle had wreaked havoc on her life a few years ago. Now Jake was trying to impose himself on her world. Although her siblings, Bridget and Bradford, didn't support her actions, they understood her need for revenge.

Her plans weren't moving as fast as she had hoped. She was a wiz with numbers and manipulated them so much that even when projects for new telecom facilities passed through all the phases, when it came down to implementing them, there was always a glitch.

When Banks Telecom's internal analysts tried to figure out what had gone wrong, they were unable to tie the issues to the false figures. As far as they were concerned, Brianna's figures were correct, and it was mismanagement on the customer's end. She used a few of these failures to plant doubt in stockholders' minds about some of the decisions Jake had been making on behalf of Banks Telecom.

She smiled for the first time since leaving Jake's office at the thought of him being berated by the main stockholders. Her smile soon faded when she saw Charles's number flash on her desk phone's screen. "Damn him," she blurted, hoping no one else heard her outburst.

Brianna opened up her top desk drawer and pulled out a bottle of aspirin. She stuck her tongue out and placed two white pills on it. She cringed as she swallowed the bitter pills without drinking any fluids.

It took a while for the pills to make her headache subside. She couldn't concentrate on work. Her mind replayed the incident in Jake's office over and over. She needed to find out more about this so-called proposal. She knew there had to be something in it for Jake, or else he wouldn't have brought it up. But what was it?

If she accepted Jake's proposal, she could convince him to share more about the business. If he trusted her with passwords, she could make it look like he was embezzling funds. Well, maybe she didn't have to take it that far; however, it would give her the leverage she needed to see

Banks Telecom fail. The more she thought about it, the more she realized the proposal could be the answer to her prayers. She didn't trust Jake; however, she had a more immediate problem to deal with—Charles.

CHAPTER 2

"Brianna turned me down. I thought I was most women's fantasy," Jake stated as he sat next to his best friend since grade school at a local bar.

After tipping the waiter, Trent turned around to face Jake. "What do you expect? That woman knows you as her boss, and then you spring something like that on her. Tact is something you're lacking."

"I like the direct approach."

"Well, if you ask me, your mental condition is hereditary."

"Man, you better be glad we're friends, or I would pop you for that comment," replied Jake.

"Just calling it like I see it. Your uncle asking you to marry some chick just to get your inheritance? Crazy, man." Trent held his drink up and took a sip. "Can't you get the money your uncle left for you another way?"

"I asked my attorney if there was a way around it, and there isn't. I need that money, or my business is going under. If I don't do something about it fast, we'll sink just like the *Titanic*."

"Do what you have to do. If it means marrying some stranger, then, by all means, do it to save the ship," advised Trent.

"Let's hope Ms. Lady comes around, or I'll be in need of a life jacket."

"How did you get yourself into this situation?"

Jake sipped his drink and paused a few seconds before answering. "I wish I knew. I thought everything was in place. My company takes the risk by investing the money and resources. All the vendors have to do is install the phone lines and towers where we tell them. Some of my vendors have been dropping the ball lately and causing some of the phone providers to not extend contracts in certain areas."

"That's bad business," noted Trent.

"Exactly. These vendors, though, are the only ones working in these areas, so my hands are tied."

"I feel for you."

The music changed from a slow jam to a more upbeat sound. Jake and Trent watched a group of women dancing on the dance floor.

"I can tell they're all high maintenance," Trent said.

"What woman isn't?"

"I'll drink to that." Trent lifted his drink up off the counter and took a sip.

"Here's to Uncle Jack." Jake drank until the glass was dry. He motioned for the bartender and ordered another round for them both.

"So tell me. What's Brianna like?" asked Trent.

Jake remembered how he felt every time his and Brianna's paths crossed. If he were to admit the truth, he would say he would have eventually asked her out on a date without his uncle's use of force. Her mere presence seemed to fill a room. He liked the way she tilted her head slightly when in deep thought and how her eyes twinkled when she found something funny. He also liked to see the fire radiating from her eyes when she got upset. That's the last thing he remembered seeing before Brianna stormed out of his office earlier that day.

He responded, "She's not bad on the eyes. I would date her."

"How do you plan on getting her to agree to marry you?"

"I'm hoping she'll do it after I throw this Mac Daddy charm on her."

Trent laughed. "What's your plan B, because from what you said, your plan A is not working."

"Ye of little faith."

"Now that's one tall drink of water. I wouldn't mind sipping from her glass," Trent said as Jake followed his gaze.

"Sure, you're right. Heads or tails," Jake said as he took out a quarter and flipped it.

"Heads."

"You lose." Jake lifted his hand to reveal the other side of the coin.

"Go for it." Trent saluted him with his glass.

Jake placed his glass on the bar and walked over near the dance floor, where the tall, slender woman with a head full of Chaka Kahn hair stood.

"Can I have this dance?" he asked and extended his hand out.

"I don't think my partner would appreciate seeing me out on the dance floor with a man," said the woman.

"Your partner?" Jake said, sounding confused.

"Yes. There she is now."

A shorter woman approached them, and he

watched as they kissed. His ego took a direct hit. "Ladies, enjoy the rest of your night," he said.

Jake didn't wait to hear their responses. He looked over in Trent's direction. Trent was laughing so hard, he almost fell out of his seat. Jake made a detour and headed for the door. He wasn't in the mood to listen to Trent anymore tonight.

He was barely in his car when his phone rang. "I don't want to hear it."

"Your chick sure knows how to dance. You should have stayed. They might be into three-somes." Trent's laughter seemed to override the loud noise in the background.

"Stop wasting my minutes." Jake clicked the phone off without waiting for Trent to respond.

Tonight he needed a little TLC, and he knew just the woman to give it to him. He scrolled through the address book on his cell phone and made a booty call.

"How could you?" Brianna yelled from the other side of the door as Charles tried to convince her to open the door to her apartment so he could get his stuff.

"Bri, you got to understand. Ten thousand dollars is a lot of money. I have my student loans and bills."

"You sold me out for ten thousand. You could have at least held out for one hundred—or a million! You're a piece of work." His words fueled her scissors as she ripped and cut the remainder of his clothes, stuffing them in a trash bag as she continued to rant. "I can't believe you agreed to break up with me for money. I should have kicked you to the curb months ago."

"Come on, baby. Open up."

At his request, she opened up the door and threw the trash bag at him, knocking him off his feet. "Screw you, Charles. Here's your stuff, and lose my number," she yelled.

"You didn't have to hit me," he whined.

Standing in the doorway, she glared at him, with rancor shooting from her eyes like fiery darts. "You better be glad that's all I did," she growled through gritted teeth.

"Come on, baby. We can still see each other on the side. He won't have to know."

Brianna now stood with one hand slapping her hip. "It was over the moment you accepted the money, so don't call me. Don't try to see me. Forget that you ever knew me."

She slammed the door. To think she had spent the last twelve months with Charles. She wasn't going to lie to herself and say she loved him, but she did care about him. She had thought she could possibly grow to love him. Fortunately for her, only her pride was hurt. Not like the time she had fallen in love with Bryon Matthews.

Brianna had met Byron her freshman year in college, and they'd been inseparable, or so she'd thought. Between working at her father's store and going to school, she had had limited free time. She'd thought Bryon understood, until she got off work earlier one night and caught him with another woman. It had broken her heart, and no matter how much Byron had begged and pleaded, she could not forgive him. She had lost not only her virginity to Byron but her heart.

The phone rang, bringing her back to the present. "I ought to make you pay for my stuff," Charles yelled on the other end.

Click. Brianna hung the phone up because she refused to listen to him. She let the rest of his calls go to voice mail. He cursed her out in each message, and she vowed to get her number changed the next day. Fortunately, she had gotten her locks changed as soon as she got home that afternoon after learning of his betrayal. She knew she shouldn't have cut up his stuff, but she had needed an outlet for her anger. Besides, she thought it was better to cut up his stuff than to stab him with the sharp scissors, which were now on the nightstand.

One problem down and another one to go. She had to figure out when the best time was to accept Jake's proposal. She had decided to accept because if they were married, his guard would be down. He would never suspect that she was behind some of his business failings.

The Banks family had haunted her and her family for the past two years because of their unscrupulous business practices. Like uncle, like nephew. If it wasn't for a Banks, her father would be alive. He wouldn't have died from a heart attack from the stress of losing his business. She had imagined herself opening up several grocery stores, but now Mayfield Groceries no longer existed, because of the greed and heartless actions of men like the Banks. Yes, the Banks would pay sooner than later. She updated her journal with the day's events, closed it up, and closed her eyes, dreaming about the ways she would make Jake squirm in and out of bed.

CHAPTER 3

Brianna waltzed into work the next day wearing her designer shades and two-piece lavender dress suit, which accentuated her long legs. She was oblivious to the stares until she reached her floor. Every time she got near someone, their conversation would cease. She knew she was looking good, but for everyone to pause in her presence, something was wrong—dead wrong.

Tosha Green, one of the few people she had befriended since working at Banks Telecom, was waiting for her at her cubicle. Tosha and Brianna had met at several social-networking events prior to Brianna working at Banks. Once she was hired, Brianna looked at Tosha as an ally and got the inside scoop on everyone from her. She trusted Tosha, but she wasn't comfortable sharing her plans about Jake with her or anyone else that worked at Banks Telecom.

"Bri, we need to talk," Tosha said while thumbing through a tech magazine.

"What's up?" Brianna could still feel eyes on

her. People would look away when she turned to look in their direction.

"Rumor has it, you got the boot. That's why everybody's surprised you're here."

"People need to mind their own business," Brianna replied as she went about her morning ritual. She hooked her laptop into the docking station on her desk and put her purse in a desk drawer.

"I knew it wasn't true, because you would have called me."

Brianna didn't respond.

Tosha asked, "You would have called me, right?"

"Of course. You would have been one of the first to know," Brianna assured her as she logged on to her computer. She glanced at the clock. "I'll meet you at break. I have a conference call I'm late for."

Tosha stood there for a few seconds before leaving Brianna's cubicle. Once Brianna was left alone, she unhooked the earpiece from her ear and went to her immediate supervisor's office. She didn't wait on an invitation to come in. She closed the door as soon as she crossed the threshold.

"Diane, is something going on I should know about?"

Diane Langston, her fifty-year-old boss, didn't wait for her to elaborate. Instead, she quickly responded, "Sorry you got caught up in the rumor mill. With the economy and layoffs blooming throughout the telecom industry, you know people will talk."

"I was just checking. I would hate to put in a full day of work only to find out I'd been fired."

"On the contrary. You're one of my best employees. In fact, you're up for a promotion. I'm just waiting to get your paperwork signed, and I was going to tell you."

Brianna sighed. "That's a relief."

Brianna turned to walk away but halted when Diane asked, "How did the meeting go?"

Brianna plastered a fake smile on her face and lied. "He wanted to commend me for my hard work."

"Really . . . I thought . . . Oh well, never mind. We shouldn't have any problems getting your promotion approved."

Brianna excused herself from Diane's office. A man carrying a huge arrangement of flowers met her at her desk. "Brianna Mayfield?" he asked.

"That's me."

"Enjoy," he responded.

"Wait," she said as she retrieved money from her purse to tip him.

He shook his hand. "No need to. It's been taken care of."

She assumed Charles had used some of his money and sent her the colorful floral arrangement to say he was sorry. She searched for the card. It read, *Sorry for yesterday. Can we start again? Meet me for lunch. A car will be waiting downstairs at one.* It was signed *J.*

A mixture of excitement and anger stirred within her. Brianna was angry at herself for feeling excited about having lunch with her self-sworn enemy. She slipped the card in her purse. She would accept his proposal, and once married, she would threaten to expose him for the fake that he was. She was sure he didn't want people to know their marriage was based on some demand his uncle had made.

Her supervisor could keep the promotion, because Brianna was going for the ultimate raise. It wouldn't bring her father back, but it would make her life a whole lot easier. Her mind went over all the things she could do with a million dollars. As a CPA, she could open up her own accounting firm or even invest in reopening Mayfield Groceries. She could be her own boss. She had a little time to think about what she would do with the money.

After working for a few hours, she met Tosha in the break room. "I want to run something past you," Brianna said as she sat across from her.

Tosha held her hand up. She was talking on her cell phone. "My girl's here. I'll call you back when I get to my desk." She flipped her phone closed. "Frank says hi."

"I don't see what you see in him."

"Don't hate. Frank knows how to put it down in and out of the bedroom." Tosha fanned herself.

"You're a freak and a gold digger rolled into one. How can you live with yourself?"

"It's not easy being me."

Brianna chuckled. "You're a mess."

"Since you're all in my Kool-Aid, what's up with Mister Charles?"

"Charles is history, so please don't say his name around me."

"And you're just now telling me? I'm upset."

Brianna looked around the break room. It didn't appear that anyone was listening. She scooted her chair closer to Tosha. "What I'm about to tell you, you have to promise me you won't tell anyone else."

"You don't trust me?"

"Promise me."

"Bri, you know I don't like making promises unless I know what it is I'm promising."

"Okay. Then I'll just keep my information to myself."

Brianna knew Tosha was going to give in, because she was the type of person who hated not being in the know. Tosha had the reputation of being the queen of drama and was a known gossiper. Brianna had purposely tested Tosha with information previously to see if she could be trusted not to repeat it. She didn't allow too many people into her inner circle, but Tosha had shown Brianna she could be trusted. Brianna hoped she wouldn't be making a wrong decision by entrusting Tosha with the information she was about to share.

Tosha's cell phone rang. "I got to take this call. It's a customer. Meet me for lunch so you can tell me the details." Tosha flipped her phone open.

"Can't. I have a lunch date," Brianna responded.

Brianna pushed her chair away from the table. Tosha motioned for her to wait.

Brianna pointed at her watch and said, "Got to go."

A few times Brianna had almost confessed to Tosha her real reasons for working at Banks. For some reason, each time she had been prepared to talk to Tosha about the company, something had interrupted them. Brianna needed someone to talk to, so she vowed to try again later.

In the meantime, Brianna had to mentally prepare herself for her lunch date with Jake. Her emotions were all over the place. Should she act the same and be her normal cheerful self or resort to the woman with an attitude, the one she had displayed during their last encounter? It all depended on Jake's actions. Her mom used to say, "You catch more bees with honey." On this day she planned on pouring it on thick.

CHAPTER 4

Jake checked his watch. It was fifteen minutes after one, and apparently, Brianna wasn't going to show up. Suddenly, the driver swung the door open, and Brianna entered the limousine before Jake could react. His eyes could not stop ogling her long legs. Why hadn't he noticed before how sleek and athletic they were? Her floral perfume attacked his senses. The fragrance wasn't familiar, but it was alluring.

"Thank you for joining me," he said as he extended his hand out.

Brianna ignored it. "Let's get one thing straight. This is just lunch."

"Of course." He picked up a bottle of champagne and poured two glasses. "Here's to a great lunch." He handed her one glass.

She took a sip and frowned. "This is nasty." She handed the glass back to him.

How could she turn her nose up at a vintage bottle of Dom Pérignon? He could kick his uncle for putting him in this predicament. He could have at least picked out a woman who knew about the finer things in life. It's obvious she didn't. They rode the rest of the way in silence.

As they rode in silence, Jake recalled reading the letter his uncle Jack's attorney had recently given him. Jake's emotions had been like a seesaw—up and down—as he'd read the letter.

I know you're wondering why I put the stipulation about marrying Brianna Mayfield in my will. Two reasons. One was to make amends with her family. What I'm about to say might make you look at me in a different light, but I hope not. Robert Mayfield, Brianna's dad, came to my bank for a loan to save his business a few years ago. We've been to the store before—Mayfield Groceries. You may recall it closing its doors a few years back.

When the loan got to the final stage of approval, I rejected it. Robert's credit was a little shaky because of the economy, but I could have approved it if I had wanted to. I didn't, because, Lord forgive me for even admitting this, Robert took my first love. His wife, Barbara, had been my first love, and I couldn't forgive him for taking her from me. Robert and I had been best friends growing up, and for him to steal my girl, well, that to me was an unforgivable act. It took me these latter years to realize that Barbara wasn't a piece of property and that I should have just let it go.

Before you think otherwise, I loved your aunt Ann like there was no tomorrow, but you know me. It may take me thirty years, but if I feel you've done me wrong, I'll get you back.

A year after I turned down Robert's loan, it seems, he lost his store. By this time, I had lost my sweet Ann. I tried to make amends with him, but he refused to listen. I offered Robert money with no interest, but he turned me down flat. I felt guilty about it and was even saddened when I learned of his death. The sight of his grief-stricken children touched something in me that I can't explain.

I learned as much as I could about the Mayfield kids. Brianna reminded me of you: determined, goal oriented, and a workaholic. Yes, your uncle thought playing matchmaker and offering money to Brianna would be like killing two birds with one stone. You would get someone to love you as much as I loved her mom and your aunt, and I could leave the Mayfields some money to try to make up for what I took from them when I refused their dad's loan.

The sound of the limousine door opening snapped Jake back into the present. The driver held the door as Brianna exited. Jake admired the voluptuous view as she exited. She was normally not his type. Although she wasn't fat, she was a little thicker than the women he usually dated. He had to admit her weight was well proportioned and in all the places that appealed to most men, including him.

Jake led them into the restaurant of the Four Seasons located in Las Colinas, one of the suburbs of Dallas, Texas. He wanted to take her to a nice restaurant and to a place where they wouldn't run into her coworkers. The maître d' led them to a table with a nice view of the villas.

"I hope this is to your satisfaction," Jake stated.

"Not bad," Brianna responded. She viewed her menu without once looking up at him.

"Order anything you like."

"I plan on it," she snapped.

His cell phone rang. It was Trent. He hit the

ignore button. Jake was used to entertaining clients from various backgrounds, but he could not get a handle on Brianna. Their last encounter hadn't ended well, so he proceeded with caution.

"So tell me. Why did you single me out for this lame proposal?" Brianna asked as they waited on their food.

"For reasons unknown to me, my uncle selected you," he lied.

"Jake, let's be honest with one another please."

"I'm trying my best."

"Try harder, because I can't see your uncle asking you to marry me without letting you know the reason."

Jake contemplated telling her about the letter. He wasn't sure he wanted to reveal it all to her at this time.

While he was thinking about what to say, Brianna said, "Tell me about your uncle, and I'm not talking about the stuff I can pull up on the Internet."

Jake smiled as he thought about his eccentric, rich uncle. The uncle who had helped put him through college and had encouraged him to get his MBA and start his own company. "Uncle Jack was a fine man. After my mother and father were killed by a drunk driver in a car accident, he took me in and raised me as his son. It's because of him that I am the man I am today."

Brianna seemed to be startled by his revelation. "Sorry to hear about your parents. What about your sisters and brothers?"

"I'm afraid I'm an only child. My uncle's wife wasn't able to have children. She died a few years ago. I think my uncle died from a broken heart.

She was the love of his life. I haven't met a woman who could compare to my aunt Ann."

"Interesting," Brianna responded. "Your uncle, it seems, was a pioneer as the only African American to own a bank in the Dallas area. Why didn't you follow in his footsteps?"

Jake said, "Uncle Jack wanted me to, but after I interned at a telecommunications company during college, my desire was to advance in that field. I worked for one of the top phone companies in the world and learned what I could. With Uncle Jack's support, I started Banks Telecom. Banks Telecom was built on the premise of us taking on jobs and doing installations that phone companies outsourced to outside vendors."

The waiter placed their plates in front of them, and the conversation slowed down. Jake picked over his food, but Brianna seemed to have a hearty appetite.

Brianna looked at Jake and then down at his plate. "You on a diet or something?"

"No. I'm not hungry."

"Hey, it was your idea to have lunch, not mine." She continued to eat her food.

He used the napkin to wipe the sweat from the palms of his hands. She was unnerving him. This was his show. He needed to get control of the situation. His business depended on it.

"Brianna, tell me about yourself," he said.

She laughed. "It's obvious you know more about me than I know about you. You knew I had a boyfriend and how to get rid of him. By the way, I do want to thank you for that." She held her glass up and tilted it his way before taking a sip of her lemonade.

"I'm sorry for intruding, but I needed to

make sure you had no reason to turn me down," he explained.

"You could have tried the old-fashioned way. You know, wine and dine and throw in a little romance."

"That would have been dishonest, and one thing you can say about Jacob Banks is that he's an honest man."

Brianna cleared her throat. "Do you always talk about yourself in the third person?"

She was grating on his nerves. He was going to call his lawyer one more time to see if there was some type of loophole to get around his uncle's will. "You must have forgotten I'm your boss."

"This isn't work-related. This is personal, and I'm the only boss when it relates to my personal affairs, so don't get it twisted," she said as she lowered her fork.

"You told me, didn't you?"

"Are we clear?" she asked.

"Absolutely." His appetite hadn't returned, but he ate, anyway.

"Now that we're clear, I need for you to tell me, Mr. Honest Jacob Banks, why your uncle wanted you to proposition me."

Jake wasn't sure how much Brianna knew about his uncle and her father's past relationship. "It seems my uncle knew your dad."

"Oh really now? How's that?"

Jake had to glance away from Brianna's accusing eyes. "The details are a little fuzzy, but apparently, Uncle Jack thought we were a good match and felt I worked too much to find a suitable wife on my own."

"Oh, I see." Brianna pulled out her compact,

looked in its mirror, and reapplied her lipstick. She looked at Jake. "I'm waiting."

This time he looked her straight in the eyes. She felt a connection with him. It had to be her imagination working overtime. She pretended to be looking at her reflection in the mirror; instead, she was avoiding eye contact.

"There's nothing more to tell. That's about it."

Brianna placed the compact back into her purse. "I want to see a copy of his will."

Her response caught him off guard. "Why would I let you see it? It's none of your b-business . . . ," he stuttered.

She looked at Jake without blinking. "Apparently, you need me. Who couldn't use a million dollars?"

"See? It would be a win-win situation for us both."

"I'm trying to work with you, Jake, so work with me, okay? I need answers."

"That's all I'm at liberty to say, Brianna."

They were at a deadlock. Brianna glanced at her watch. "If we don't hurry back, I'll be late for a conference call, so let's table this discussion until you can show me a will."

Jake thought she had conceded at first; however, he wasn't too sure when she winked her eye and got up from the table. He left a hundred-dollar bill to cover their meal and the tip before rushing to catch up with Brianna. The limousine driver opened the door for them. Jake waited for Brianna to enter the limo first.

She turned around and looked him in the eyes. "No staring at my butt, either."

Jake couldn't resist and chuckled before he could control himself. Now he had to figure out a way not to show her the will. She did not need to know the details of his uncle's past transgressions. Fortunately, the contents of the letter were not in the will. If she found out the details, there's no telling how she would react. He didn't want to be around to find out, either.

CHAPTER 5

Brianna didn't like how lunch had gone. She tried to maintain her control by putting up a barrier. It was beginning to get hard to do so, because every time Jake looked at her, she felt like he could see straight to her soul. Maybe going through this charade wasn't worth it.

The ride back to the office was just like the ride over to the restaurant. Neither one of them said a thing. The music blasted from the speakers. They were both in their own world.

When the limousine pulled up in front of the office building, Jake reached into his jacket pocket and removed some papers and handed them to her. "If you'll look over this contract and sign it, we can move forward to the next stage."

Brianna took the papers and placed them in her purse. "I'll have my attorney look these over and get back with you." When Jake just stared at her, she added, "You didn't think I was going to sign something without reading it, did you?"

He cleared his throat. "Well . . . no. I just

thought if you were going to agree to it, you would just sign, and we could go on to the next step."

Brianna leaned in closer to him. "Since you've had me thoroughly checked out, you should know I'm also thorough and proficient." She kissed him on the cheek.

She didn't wait for the driver. She opened her door herself and left Jake sitting in the limousine, speechless. Not certain if he was watching or not, she made sure she added a few twists in her walk.

The security guard whistled as she entered the lobby. "Brianna, you better stop that before you catch something you don't want," he teased.

"Mark, don't have me tell your wife," Brianna joked.

"Aw now, why do you want to bring her up?" asked Mark.

Brianna laughed. Mark was old enough to be her dad, but he tried hard to hold on to his youth. She admitted he kept himself in good shape. He looked ten years younger than his fifty-seven years. She always threatened to tell his wife about his flirting.

The elevator doors opened, and to her luck, Tosha was on the elevator. "Girl, I've been looking all over for you."

"I had a lunch date." Brianna looked smug.

"Details. You got rid of Charles and got a new man already?"

Brianna opened her mouth to talk but shut it when Jake entered the elevator. "Ladies," he said.

Tosha exchanged greetings with him. Brianna didn't. She nodded her head instead.

Tosha, not one to be intimidated by the boss,

continued their conversation. "So tell me about your lunch date. Is he fine?"

Brianna glanced at Jake. He was looking in her direction. She responded, "He'll do."

Jake looked like he wanted to say something. Brianna smiled.

"Well, if he's not fine, does he at least have a good job?" asked Tosha.

"Oh, he's definitely rolling in the dough. He throws away money like it's growing on trees," replied Brianna.

"I hear you," said Tosha.

"You know how we do. No romance without finance." Brianna purposely gave Tosha some dap. The elevator stopped on their floor. She said, "Have a nice day, Mr. Banks."

Jake didn't respond. Brianna made sure Tosha wasn't looking before she turned around and blew him a kiss. The elevator doors shut.

Tosha grabbed her arm and pulled her toward the break room. "Girl, he was looking at you like you were syrup and he wanted to slop you up like a biscuit."

"Please. I'm not his type."

"I can't tell. If I were you, I would go for it."

She had Brianna's full attention. "Would you really? I mean, he is the CEO, and you know it's taboo to mess with someone where you make your money."

"Girl, this is the new millennium. If he's interested, I say work your magic and reel him in."

"He is a cutie."

"And fine. Don't forget fine. I could get lost in his sexy gray eyes all day and night."

It was the perfect opportunity to let Tosha know about his proposition, but she couldn't take the chance of Tosha letting it slip to someone else. She opted not to divulge the information. She glanced at her watch. "Girl, enough talk about men. I'm already running late. I'll talk with you later." Brianna left Tosha in the break room and went back to her desk. She sniffed the flowers on her desk and smiled.

She pulled out the papers Jake had handed her and read them over. She used to work in a law office and had kept in touch with a few of the lawyers. She contacted one of them to see if they could review the papers. She hung up and faxed a copy of the papers over to the lawyer. She waited to receive the fax confirmation before returning to her desk.

Her mind was on her current project, specifically, figuring out how to hire resources with the customer's limited budget. Brianna's e-mail indicator sounded, alerting her that she had a new e-mail. She glanced over her shoulder to make sure no one was coming up behind her. She retrieved the e-mail and reviewed it. According to Brianna's lawyer friend, the only loophole in the contract involved her being caught sleeping with another man. Otherwise, they were only required to stay married one year, and then she would be a millionaire, and he could go on about his business. There wasn't any stipulation that they had to consummate the marriage.

Could she go ahead with it? She would have a year to make it appear that Jake was mismanaging funds. If people knew their marriage was a sham, Jake could possibly lose his credibility that way as well. There was no telling what else Jake was hiding, so being married to him, she would have access to his home, and she would be able to discover other skeletons, if he had any. The fact that he would pay someone off to manipulate a situation was enough for her to see how similar he was to his uncle.

She weighed the pros and cons of signing the contract. She would have easy access to information and funds, or so she hoped. She could temporarily live the life of a rich socialite. She would have one of the most eligible bachelors in the Dallas–Fort Worth area at her mercy. What she didn't like about the situation was there was no romance, and she had never thought she would marry someone she wasn't in love with. If he were alive, how would her father feel about her marrying a Banks? He wouldn't be too happy about it. She asked herself again if she could go through with it.

She typed up a few amendments to be added to the original contract. After having her friend check the wording, she felt it was time to go see Jake. She asked herself, if Jake agreed to her amendments, would she or wouldn't she agree to marry him? She placed the papers in a folder and headed to the fourteenth floor to give Jake her answer.

CHAPTER 6

Brianna held the folder with the contract in one hand and used her other hand to open the glass door leading to Jake's office on the fourteenth floor. "I don't have an appointment with Mr. Banks, but he wanted me to hand deliver this file."

Joan, Jake's secretary, looked over the rim of her glasses. Brianna assumed she was used to women making excuses to see him. "You can leave it here with me, and I'll make sure he gets it."

"He told me to make sure I put it in his hands, and I don't want to piss off the boss."

Joan called Jake before giving Brianna a response. "He'll be here shortly. You can wait in his office."

"Thank you," Brianna responded.

Brianna was drawn to the bookcase when she entered Jake's office. They appeared to have similar tastes when it came to books. A Chester Himes novel was a little out of place, so she assumed he must have read it recently. The back cover of the book had her entranced, so when Jake entered the room, it caught her a little off guard.

"I hope this is good news," Jake said.

She turned around. "Close the door and I'll tell you."

Brianna watched Jake do as she commanded and waited for him to walk over to where she was standing. His walk was like that of a panther on the prowl, and she was his prey. She retreated and took a seat across from his desk before he could reach her. She sat back and crossed her legs.

Jake took a seat across from her. Brianna handed him the folder. "If you can agree with my amendments, we might have a deal."

Brianna watched Jake read her list of amendments. His facial expressions didn't reveal if he was for or against the changes she'd made. Brianna shifted in her seat as she waited for Jake to respond.

"Some of these are reasonable, like paying off your student loan. But making sure you have fresh flowers once a week? Come on now." Jake placed the papers down in front of him.

"I'm a sucker for flowers, but you know that, don't you?"

"Actually, I didn't. But I'll make a mental note of it."

"Do more than that. Just make sure I get a fresh arrangement of flowers every week, and we'll be fine."

He looked back at the list. "What's this about no chocolate? I thought all women loved chocolate."

"Well, I'm not all women. The only thing chocolate I like is my men." She leaned back and winked at him.

He stared at her for a few seconds before looking back at the list. He said, "I don't like pets. They are too messy."

"I haven't had a dog since I lived with my parents, and since we'll be living together, you really need to reconsider."

"I'll think about it."

Brianna knew some of the things were little nuisances. She had added those on purpose. She wanted to see how serious Jake was about her becoming his wife. She admitted there was something alluring about him. If his uncle hadn't been the object of her hatred for the past few years, she would have found Jake attractive.

"Separate bedrooms? Come on now. We're going to be together for a year. We can at least have a little fun," Jake teased.

"I suggest you invest in some petroleum jelly and videos because this"—she placed her hand on her chest—"this is off-limits."

"You can't blame me for trying."

She rolled her eyes. "Whatever."

He continued to go through the items on the list. "I can't agree with number twenty."

"If you want me to sign the contract, you will."

Brianna could see the sweat forming on his forehead. She refused to back down, though. She wanted to know why his uncle had mentioned her in his will. She leaned forward in her chair, awaiting his response.

He conceded. "Look. Like I said when I first propositioned you, my uncle left me some money. For reasons unknown to me, he insisted I marry first before getting access to it."

"But why me? That's what I don't understand."

"I told you. He knew your father. Apparently, he felt you and I would make a good couple. If I knew more than that, I would tell you."

"Let me see the will. Let me see where he said you had to marry *me* specifically."

Brianna waited for him to retrieve the will from his locked desk drawer. He flipped through the pages before handing it to her.

She read it until she saw her name mentioned.

While she was reading, Jake said, "Truthfully, I don't know why Uncle Jack insisted it be you. You seem to have brains and beauty all rolled into one, but you're not my type."

Brianna didn't know if she should be offended or happy. "You're not my type, either, so we have something else in common."

"I didn't mean for it to come out like that."

"No need to mince words." She leaned back in her chair and continued to read the will. She glanced up and asked, "If I'm not your type, why don't you forfeit the money?"

"I can't afford to."

Brianna placed the will on the desk. "Not you." She glanced at the plaques on the wall. "According to the *Dallas Morning News,* your business is booming."

"You work in accounting. You know what we're facing."

"I'm not the chief financial officer, so, no, Mr. Banks, I don't."

"Let me inform you. What I'm about to tell you should not leave this room."

Brianna used her finger and crossed her heart.

Jake continued. "Banks Telecom is on the brink of financial trouble. If we don't get a handle on the vendors and do more in the research and development area, we could be facing layoffs, and God forbid, I'm forced into bankruptcy. I would have to shut the doors."

Things were worse than Brianna had thought. She might not need the entire year to see Banks Telecom fail. For a moment, she felt guilty about her part in setting it all in motion.

"I've had my attorney look through the will, and it clearly states that it has to be you," Jake added.

Karma was something. Her father had lost his business when Jake's uncle wouldn't approve a loan that could have saved it. Now here she sat, holding an ace. Brianna could turn Jake down, and he could lose it all, just like her dad. She contemplated whether or not to tear up the signed contract she held.

Then she thought about having financial freedom, freedom to start her own business and be her own boss. *I should be holding out for more money. A million dollars. Hmm.* Brianna placed her index finger on her chin. "I don't think your original offer is enough. Up the ante to five mill, and we have a deal."

Jake's eyes turned a darker shade of gray. "You're something else."

"No. I'm a businesswoman." She grabbed their contract, took the pen from his desk, and went through the document, changing the dollar amount to five million dollars, initialing it, and signing it. "Here's your signed contract."

CHAPTER 7

Jake looked at the contract and then back at Brianna. What was he getting himself into? He could tell she wasn't going to make this easy for him. It was going to be a long year. He would do anything to save his company, but this was uncalled for. He could understand Uncle Jack wanting to make amends with someone he felt he had wronged, but he couldn't understand why he had set up this crazy arrangement.

His back was up against the wall. He didn't bother to look at the other amendments on her list. "I accept your conditions. It's a deal." He extended his hand across the desk.

"Looks like it's a win-win situation for both of us," Brianna responded.

He ignored the jolt that went through his body when their hands touched. When she smiled, her dimples appeared deeper than what he remembered.

"Brianna, you don't know how much I appreciate you doing me this favor."

"Yeah. Whatever."

"I'm serious. Even though I think the money is more than enough, you still could have turned me down."

"Remember that when you find yourself frustrated."

"In the words of Rodney King, can't we just get along?"

She stood up. "As long as you remember the rules. Like item number twenty-five."

"Item number twenty-five?" Jake picked up the sheet of paper with her list on it.

"I suggest you tell all your women that you're no longer on the market."

"B-but . . . ," he stuttered.

"If I'm going to be your wife, I will not stand for it. Besides, if I can't have me a man on the side, there's no way I'm going to be the only one going without."

"You're a tough one."

"I'm about equality."

He followed her to the door. "I'll be in touch," he said before opening the door.

Jake watched her walk away. He was hypnotized and didn't immediately notice Joan staring at him. He knew it was only a matter of time before he would have to let her know about his upcoming nuptials. For now, he had to deal with telling the women in his life he would be unavailable for a year. He had a healthy sexual appetite, and he didn't particularly like this new part of their agreement. But he had to do whatever it took to save Banks Telecom. If it meant going without sex for a year, he would have to make the sacrifice, no matter how difficult it would be. And it would be difficult. His hormones were raging now, and he blamed one woman—Brianna Mayfield.

In the meantime, Jake had a company to save. With the signed contract, he would gain access to some of his uncle's money. He needed to get the papers to his attorney pronto, and he wouldn't depend on a courier. He decided to deliver them himself.

Two hours later Jake found himself sitting across the dinner table, with Heidi. She was five ten and an ex-model who now ran her own day spa. They were not only lovers, but they were friends, or so he had thought until he felt the slap on his left cheek and the glass of wine splashed on his face and, ultimately, in his lap.

"I've wasted two years of my life trying to get you to commit, and you tell me you're marrying some other woman. The hell with you," she yelled, then stormed out of the restaurant, leaving him to the embarrassing stares of the other patrons.

The waiter rushed over to his table. "Sir, let me get that for you."

"No, I got it," said Jake as he wiped up as much of the wine as he could. He paid the waiter and rushed out of the restaurant. He was embarrassed as people passed by and glanced at the wet spots on his shirt and pants as he waited on the valet to pull his car around.

Jake called Trent as soon as he got in the car and told him about Heidi's actions. "Man, for someone so smart, you're stupid," Trent said on the other end.

"I thought telling her in a public place would make it easier."

"Well, I hate to hear what happens when you tell Samantha. Now that one there, she might slash your tires."

"Don't remind me. I'll be doing the rest through phone calls, because frankly, I don't believe in laying hands on a woman, but I'm not going to stand for another one putting their hands on me."

"Pretty boy, get over it. You deserved the slap."

"Whose side are you on?" asked Jake.

"Man, you know I always have your back."

"I can't tell."

Samantha was waiting for him in his driveway when he pulled up. "It's about time you showed up," she said as she exited her car, wearing nothing but a trench coat.

Jake wondered whether or not she was fully exposed, or if she was wearing some sexy lingerie. He would break it off with her, but not until afterward. He needed to get this one last escapade out of the way, and sexy Samantha was the perfect one to oblige him. Jake would deal with telling Samantha about his upcoming nuptials later. He rolled down his window. "I admit it. I forgot."

"I should just go home and make you suffer," Samantha teased.

"I would hate for you to have made a wasted trip."

They were barely in the house before their lips locked. Jake's member wouldn't respond. What was wrong with him? He decided it had to be stress.

"Why don't you meet me in the living room?" he said.

"Don't keep me waiting too long," Samantha purred.

Jake watched her walk away. Samantha's brown thighs were revealed as the trench coat swung open as she pranced out of the room. All he could do was shake his head. He was thankful the lights were dim and she hadn't noticed the stains on his clothes. He went upstairs and changed clothes.

Samantha's back was turned to him when he entered the living room. She turned around and let the coat drop, showcasing her nude body. They met each other midway and had a groping session. Jake wanted Samantha, but his body betrayed him. After a few more minutes of kissing, he pushed her away and led her to the couch.

"There's something I need to tell you," he said, reneging on what he had told Trent earlier. He had decided to face Samantha head-on.

Samantha sat naked, facing him, with a strange expression on her face. "We can talk later."

He got up and retrieved her coat. "Put this on first."

"I know how to get your johnson working," she responded. She threw the coat to the side. She reached over to touch him, but he blocked her hand.

"Sam, talk. We need to talk."

"Look, Jake. I didn't come over here for talking. If I wanted talking, I would have called up my boyfriend. I want you and I want you now."

"That's just it. My body isn't cooperating, and there's a reason for it. I don't know how else to say this."

"Just say it," she blurted.

Jake rubbed his two hands together, preparing himself for the inevitable. He was prepared to block any hand movements. "What we're doing has to stop. I'm getting married."

Samantha laughed. "Is that all? Is that why you can't get it up? You're feeling guilty. Dear, I never wanted a commitment from you. I just want you."

Jake felt relieved. "Cool. Then there's no problem. Put your coat on, and I'll walk you to the door."

"No. It's all good. I wish you luck."

Samantha put her coat on and walked out of his house. She was calm. Too calm. But he wasn't going to complain. That had ended without any drama, unlike earlier tonight. After making sure Samantha had left, he opted to just avoid the other women he had dated. He would let them know if they called; otherwise, he was going to avoid them as long as he could.

CHAPTER 8

It was Friday night, and Brianna hadn't talked to Jake since she'd handed him those papers on Wednesday. She tried calling him, but his secretary claimed he was out of the office. That was fine. He knew how to reach her. In the meantime, she planned to meet her siblings for their monthly outing.

Telling her sister and brother about Jake wasn't going to be easy, but she didn't want them to find out from someone else. With Jake the CEO of a major company in the Dallas–Fort Worth area, it wouldn't be long before the news swept through the society pages.

Brianna paused outside of Bridget's door before knocking. She took a few deep breaths and knocked. Matt, Bridget's husband, answered the door. She hugged her tall and handsome brother-in-law.

"They're in the back," Matt said after kissing her on the cheek.

"Thanks. So how are you?" she asked as she followed him to the den.

"I'm thinking about switching jobs. There are rumors of layoffs, so I'm not waiting around to find out."

"I don't blame you."

Brianna, at thirty-four, was two years older than Bridget and a few shades lighter. She greeted her sister with a hug.

"You're late," Bridget said.

"Traffic," Brianna responded.

Bradford, their younger brother, sat in the corner, on the phone. He kept his hair closely shaven. On this night, his head was bald, and the light reflected off his perfectly round brown head. He threw his hand up and waved to acknowledge Brianna's presence. She walked over to where he sat and bent down to hug and kiss him on the cheek.

Bridget commented, "He's going to die with that phone next to his ear."

Before Brianna could add her comment, Bradford disconnected his phone call and said, "I can't help it. I'm popular."

"Your player ways will catch up with you one day," Bridget said.

"All of us can't be like you. Settle down and have the house and white picket fence, with a dog named Spot," Bradford pointed out.

"My dog's name is Doodles," Bridget reminded.

Bradford looked at Brianna. "Spot. Doodles. Whatever."

"Why do I always have to play referee?" Brianna asked as she plopped down on the sofa and crossed her legs.

"Because some folks refuse to grow up," Bridget responded.

Bradford scooted up to the end of his chair. "You better be glad I don't hit women."

Brianna intervened. "Look. If this is all you're going to do, I'm leaving. Now apologize to each other."

They each mumbled something under their breath before saying, "I'm sorry."

"All this refereeing has gotten me hungry. What's for dinner?" asked Brianna.

"Come on. The food's ready," said Bridget.

Brianna looped her arm through her brother's, and they followed Bridget into the kitchen. "My favorite," Bradford stated as they each took turns washing their hands in the kitchen sink.

"I was in the mood for Italian," Bridget replied as she handed each one of them a plate.

"Me too," Brianna said as she piled her plate high with lasagna and salad.

Matt got his dinner but didn't join them at the dinner table. The conversation remained light as they ate. Brianna went back and forth in her head, contemplating her approach to revealing the upcoming nuptials to Jake.

"Matt and I are having a baby," Bridget blurted.

It took a few seconds for it to register. Bradford offered his congratulations first. Brianna followed. "Congratulations, sis. I know how much you want kids."

"We've been trying for over a year now, and I found out earlier today," Bridget revealed.

Brianna reached for Bridget's hand and squeezed it.

Bradford said, "I don't have a big announcement like that, but I am dating this twenty-six-year-old. She might be the one to make me settle down."

Brianna rolled her eyes. "You said the same thing about the forty-year-old last month."

"Yes. Well, she tried to control me, and I'm not one to be tamed," he replied.

Bridget and Brianna both laughed. Brianna listened as her thirty-year-old brother discussed his active dating life. One thing about Bradford, he didn't discriminate when it came to age or race. She doubted the twenty-six-year-old would be around long, but it was entertaining to listen to him.

Bradford switched gears and said, "I read on the Internet that Banks Telecom might be in some financial trouble."

"Good," Bridget responded. "Now they'll see how Dad felt."

Brianna knew this was the opening she needed. It was either now or never. "I have a major announcement to make myself."

Bridget and Bradford ignored her and continued to talk about Banks Telecom.

Bradford said, "I still think Brianna was crazy for taking a job there."

"Me too," Bridget said. "Jake Banks is probably just like his uncle."

"Folks don't get ahead in business by being nice, so I'm sure he is," Bradford commented.

Irritated, Brianna took her fork and tapped her glass with it, which got their attention. "I said I have an announcement to make."

"Don't get your feathers ruffled," Bridget said.

"Before I tell you, promise me you'll hear me out first," Brianna told them.

Bradford said, "We're listening."

"Charles and I broke up," Brianna confessed.

Bridget clapped her hands. "Glad you finally wised up."

Brianna looked at Bradford, but he didn't have any extra commentary. Her breathing got heavier. "I've accepted Jacob Banks's proposal. We're getting married."

Bradford spit out his drink. Brianna handed him a napkin. Bridget sat speechless.

Bradford yelled, "Are you crazy? How could you sleep with the enemy?"

"You're going to dishonor our father's memory by marrying him! I told you working at his company would be disastrous," Bridget yelled.

Matt rushed into the room. "What's going on in here?"

Bridget's face turned beet red. "My sister has informed us, she's getting married."

Matt wrapped his arm around Bridget's shoulders. "Well, congrats."

Bridget pulled away and stormed out of the room. "She's a traitor."

Matt followed behind her.

Bradford said, "Always the drama queen."

"If you two would have let me explain before overreacting, I would have told you why I agreed to marry him."

"I'm waiting." Bradford leaned back in his chair.

Bridget now stood in the doorway, with her arms crossed. Brianna responded, "His business is crumbling, and he needs me."

Bridget said, "Matt, get me the phone. I'm calling Charter Forest right now. She needs to be admitted to the psych ward."

"I'm not crazy," Brianna declared.

"Three against one says you are," Bradford said.

Matt said, "Hey, I'm not in this."

"Matt! Well, it's two against one. Majority rules," Bridget added.

Brianna stood up. "I knew telling you about this was a bad idea."

Bradford poured himself a drink. "I don't trust him or anyone else with the last name Banks. Why do you have to marry him?"

"I can't say right now. I just need you two to trust me," replied Brianna.

Bridget and Bradford mumbled between themselves. Brianna couldn't understand what they were saying. Bradford was the first to address her. "If you feel this is something you need to do, I'll support you."

"Can you convince Bridget to do the same?" asked Brianna.

Bradford took big gulps of his drink. "You're on your own."

CHAPTER 9

Jake attempted to keep a low profile over the weekend. He spent it by himself, going over his personal and professional life. He wasn't satisfied with either. He hoped the decision to live out the last will and testament of his uncle would be fruitful in all areas.

Monday mornings were usually filled with meetings, but Joan informed him several people had cancelled. He read an article online about the rumors about his company. He had hoped news about the company's financial woes wouldn't get out, and soon he would have to address the rumors. For now, he had a woman to romance, or pretend to romance at least.

"Joan, can you get Brianna on the line?" he asked over the intercom.

"I sure will," she responded. Less than a minute later, she announced, "She's on line one."

"Bri. It is okay if I call you Bri, isn't it?" he asked in a cheerful voice.

"I would prefer if you called me Brianna," she responded.

"Did you miss me?"

"Like a wart," Brianna told him.

"Ouch. You're bad for the ego."

"I aim to please."

"I called you to ask you to lunch and also to ask you to inform your supervisor you'll be in a meeting with me the second half of your day."

"What project are we supposedly working on?"

"I'm sure you'll come up with something. You seem to be very creative. Look, I have a meeting to go to. I'll have a car waiting for you at one. Same place as before."

Jake refused to wait for her to respond and disconnected the call. Brianna wasn't one to be bossed around, and he actually found the trait attractive. He needed to watch himself around her. The thought of her had caused him not to be able to perform last week with Samantha.

In between meetings, Joan pulled him aside. "There's more going on between you and Brianna, isn't there?" she asked.

Jake closed the door to the conference room before responding. "I trust that what I tell you won't leave this room."

"Of course not."

"You're one of the few people that know about the financial state of our company. Brianna is the key to helping us save it."

"I don't understand."

"I really shouldn't be telling you this, but I trust you. Uncle Jack left me some money. However, it comes with conditions—one being that I marry Brianna Mayfield."

"She's smart, she's beautiful, and she's feisty. I think you've met your match in Ms. Mayfield."

"For some reason you don't seem as surprised as I thought you would be," Jake observed.

"As you know, I was good friends with both your aunt and your uncle. I'm sure your uncle wouldn't have added that clause without a good reason."

"Brianna has been one of my best employees, but as my woman, I don't know how that's going to work out."

"I've seen you two together. There's some chemistry there."

"Sparks of conflict."

Joan laughed. "Two competitive spirits coming together makes for an interesting relationship."

"No comment. I am concerned about what the employees are going to say when I announce our engagement."

"I'll handle any backlash. Don't worry yourself with it."

"Thanks, Joan."

Jake felt relieved that Joan would be supportive of this new phase of his life. The rest of the morning went by fast. He called his driver and waited in the limousine for Brianna to arrive. He wrapped up his call when Brianna took a seat next to him.

"How is your day going?" he asked.

"Busy, but manageable," she responded as she flipped open her cell phone. "I'll call you back," she said into her phone, then looked back at him. "Now what were you saying?"

"Nothing but how beautiful your dimples are when you smile."

"I guess I'll have to stop smiling when I'm around you then."

"You won't be able to resist. I've been told I have a great sense of humor."

"That was from women who were trying to impress you. Me, you can count on me telling you the truth."

Jake moved closer to her. "That's good to hear. We'll be spending a lot of time together over the next year, so I look forward to hearing the truth for the next three hundred and sixty-five days."

"You can count on it."

His cell phone vibrated. He glanced at the caller ID display. It was Trent. He needed a diversion, so he answered. "Jacob speaking."

"Oh, you're trying to act like it's business. You're with a client or your new love?"

"No, I'm not with a client right now. I'm going to lunch. How may I help you?"

"I'll let you get back to your lunch. I was checking to see what happened to you this weekend."

"I'll call you back." Jake hung up the phone. He turned his attention toward Brianna, only to notice her staring at him. It made him uncomfortable. He couldn't think of anything to say to her. He turned up the volume on the stereo and poured himself a drink.

"That was rude. You could have offered me something to drink," she snapped.

"The last time I did, you handed it back to me, letting me know it was 'nasty.'"

Brianna rolled her eyes. "I'm sure the bar is stocked with other stuff besides overrated champagne."

She reached over him, and the strawberry scent in her hair filled his nostrils. Her breasts grazed his leg, and his body reacted. He hoped she didn't look down, or she would be in for a surprise. Brianna pulled open the door to the minibar and picked up a cold soda.

"Bri?"

"Brianna."

"Excuse me. Brianna. Why the attitude?"

"I don't have an attitude."

"Yes, you do."

She opened her drink and took a sip. "No, I don't."

"I don't want to argue with you."

"You're the only one arguing."

Before Jake realized it, he had leaned over toward Brianna and kissed her. Their lips locked, and instead of pushing him away, she invited his tongue inside her mouth. He slipped his tongue inside her mouth, and he could hear her gasp, or was he gasping? They were entangled with one another, oblivious to the limousine stopping. The sunlight streaming through the limo door the driver had opened ended their tongue entanglement.

Brianna brushed her fingers across her lips. Jake attempted to straighten out his pants before exiting. He thought of something disgusting to get his body to deactivate the desire that coursed through it. To think it was only a kiss. He had to get a grip on himself and fight this physical attraction.

Neither spoke to the other during the first part of lunch. Brianna was the first to break the ice. "Why did you do that?"

"You wouldn't shut up," he responded.

"Let's not make this more complicated than it has to be."

"Why don't we go with the flow and see where it goes?"

"No. We have an agreement. We're to display affection only when in the open, but otherwise, its hands off."

"That's not something I agreed to."

"Check out your list. It's number twenty-eight."

"We might need to renegotiate, because that list of yours is going to keep me in trouble."

Brianna chuckled. Jake found himself smiling, too.

CHAPTER 10

Brianna didn't want to admit it, but she found Jake charming. The kiss. As soon as his lips had touched hers, she'd melted. *Girl, you need to get a grip on yourself. You can't fall for his charm. He's slick. Remember that. Stay in control,* she told herself as she sipped on her iced tea. She lost control when she saw the twinkle in his eyes. She needed something stronger than iced tea, but it was only lunchtime.

Jake's mouth moved, but she didn't hear a word coming out of it. She was thinking about the kiss once again. She had been with Charles for an entire year, and not once had he made her feel the way Jake had with a simple kiss.

"So is that fine?" Jake asked.

"Sorry. Can you repeat what you just said?"

"Are you okay?" he asked, sounding concerned.

"Yes. Of course." She took her iced tea and drank it until the only thing left was ice.

"I think we should have an engagement party. I don't know if I should make the announcement on the invitations or wait until everyone shows up for the party."

"When are you talking about having this party?"

"Soon. Because the wedding is going to be in the next six weeks."

"Six weeks? I don't have time to plan a wedding in six weeks."

"You don't have to plan anything. Joan will find a wedding planner to take care of everything for you."

"Fine. But back to this engagement party. Have you told Joan about our arrangement?"

Jake looked away. "Yes. I had to."

"But I thought we were supposed to keep this between the two of us. How am I going to face her, knowing she knows?" Brianna clenched her teeth.

"Calm down. Joan can be trusted. She's not going to tell anybody else."

"You know what? Maybe we should avoid it altogether. It's nobody's business what we do, and having this party could lead to a lot of questions. Questions that neither one of us would want to answer."

"I would say to hell with the party, but the party is needed. It's the proper protocol for a man in my position."

"I'll agree only if you don't put the fact that it's an engagement party on the invitations. Let it be a surprise."

"I can do that. I'll get Joan on it right away." He sent Joan a quick text message. He looked up and said, "I just thought about it. Things might change for you at work."

"I'm prepared. Folks are already speculating that I'm about to get fired, since I've been summoned to your office several times recently."

"Why haven't you said anything?"

"I'm a big girl. I can handle my own problems."

"Bri, you have me now. We're a team."

"If we're a team, why don't I have all your contact information? I have your cell number and your office number, but what's your home number?" Brianna asked.

He reached into his pocket and pulled out a business card and pen and wrote on the back of the card. He handed it to her. "This is all my contact information, including my home address."

She looked the card over before placing it in her purse. "I would give you my information, but you already have it all."

"I do, but you don't have to be so cold about it."

"Let's get one thing straight before we go any further." She pointed at herself. "This is me. What you see is what you get. You can either deal with it or void the contract."

"I like what I see. You're a little difficult at times, but I can handle you."

"We'll see about that."

Brianna had to admit, Jake turned her on. Since they would be spending more time together, she might as well enjoy it. She wanted to see him squirm. She turned on her charm and flirted with him during the rest of lunch.

By the time dessert arrived, both of them were full from the three-course meal. If it was a real date, she would have appreciated the ambiance of the Four Seasons. The duck pond caught her eye from where they were sitting. She saw a few couples holding hands and walking, enjoying one another's company. She felt a twinge of jealousy. Looking across at Jake, she wondered if under different circumstances, it would have been possible between the two of them.

"A penny for your thoughts," Jake said.

"More like a quarter. Inflation, man," she responded, flashing a smile. Her dimples deepened.

"What else would you like to do today?"

"I'm yours for the rest of the day. I told my supervisor I would be with you in a meeting."

"I forsee a meeting at Six Flags."

"I'm not dressed for an amusement park."

"There's a remedy for that. There's a boutique here." He pulled out an American Express card and handed it to her. "Go find yourself something nice. I have a few business calls to make. I'll meet you in the lobby when you're through."

"I guess there are perks with dating the boss." She placed the card in her wallet.

Less than an hour later, Brianna was dressed in a pair of designer jeans with rhinestones of various colors on the pockets and a pink shirt with matching rhinestones. She had exchanged her heels for a pair of white designer tennis shoes. The salesclerk placed her other clothes in a bag. After paying with Jake's American Express, she left the boutique in search of Jake.

Jake shook a man's hand before turning to meet her near the door. He leaned down and kissed her on the forehead. "You look good."

Brianna tried her best not to be taken aback by his public display of affection.

"Don't act like you don't know me," someone yelled.

"Who is that?" she asked.

"Nobody. Just keep on walking," Jake said as he tried to rush her through the door.

"Jake!" The woman said his name loud enough for several people to hear.

Brianna stopped and turned around. Jake had no choice at this point and followed suit. Before he responded, the tall woman was standing right in front of them.

"Samantha," Jake said.

"Nice seeing you here." She looked at Brianna. "Is this the fiancée you told me about?"

Jake cleared his throat. "Yes. Brianna. Samantha."

Samantha reached her hand out to shake Brianna's hand. Brianna had a firm handshake. She wanted Samantha to know she wasn't a pushover. She looked her straight in the eyes until Samantha looked away.

"Congratulations and good luck," said Samantha.

"We don't need luck. We have each other," replied Brianna as she reached for Jake's hand and squeezed it. Jake leaned down and kissed her lightly on the lips.

Samantha rolled her eyes. "Well, I see you two are in a hurry, so I don't want to keep you."

"Nice meeting you, Sam," Brianna responded. "Dear, we don't want to be late." She grabbed Jake's hand and walked to the waiting limousine. Once they were seated, she said, "Your little girlfriend didn't seem too happy running into us."

"Sam's never been a girlfriend."

"Oh, really now? That's not the vibe I got. Fess up."

Brianna enjoyed watching him squirm. Women knew the difference between a friend and a lover, and Samantha's actions proved her role in Jake's life. Brianna leaned back in the seat and crossed her arms.

"She and I used to kick it."

Brianna burst into laughter. "Why do you men do that? Why can't you just come out and say you had a sexual relationship without commitment?"

"Because."

"It is what it is."

"What kind of relationship did you and Charles have?"

Brianna's smile faded. "Charles is off-limits."

"Did you love him?"

"No, and for the second time, Charles is off-limits."

"Any man who would take money to dump a woman is a punk in my book. You're better off without him."

"Are you any better? You offered the money."

"I'm a man willing to pay whatever amount for what I want and, Ms. Mayfield, I want you."

CHAPTER 11

Jake meant exactly what he said. He wanted Brianna, and before the year ended, he planned on making her his in every sense of the word. Her little gesture in front of Samantha had made him realize one thing: she took their little arrangement seriously.

"I'll call you when we're ready," Jake told the driver. He looked over at Brianna. "So are you ready to have some fun?"

They spent the next few hours at Six Flags amusement park, riding rides and eating. They both were exhausted by the time the driver pulled up outside of the gate. Jake placed in the limo the items Brianna had bought and the stuffed animals he'd won by spending lots of money on games.

"See, I'm not too bad to hang around with," Jake commented.

"The verdict is still out."

"Come on. Admit it," he teased.

Brianna rolled her eyes. "Surprisingly, hanging out with you wasn't too bad."

"You're not being fair."

"The male ego is so fragile. Jake, I had fun. Is that fair enough?" Brianna asked as she moved her head around.

"Let me." He massaged her shoulders. "See, it didn't hurt you to admit that."

She let out a few ahs. "That feels good."

Her moans tempted him so much so that he wanted to kiss the back of her neck. He refrained. She stopped him and turned back around in her seat.

"Why don't you let me drop these things off at your place, and then we can go back to get your car?" he asked.

"Sounds like a plan to me. I really don't want folks all in my business."

"If anyone gives you a hard time, let me know."

"You should know by now I can take care of myself."

Jake grabbed Brianna's hand, and before she could react, he brought it up to his lips and kissed the back of it. "I'm here if you need me."

"If I thought you were really sincere, I would let you kiss me."

"But I am."

"In that case, what are you waiting for?"

Jake didn't know if Brianna was serious or setting him up to let him down. He opted to not take the chance. His libido couldn't stand too much more teasing. "What about the rule on your list?"

"Chicken." Brianna made some clucking sounds.

"I got your chicken."

This time when he kissed her, he didn't hold anything back. She reached her arms around his neck and pulled him closer. It took all the restraint he could muster not to rip off her clothes.

He pulled back, and she gently wiped the lipstick from his lips.

Jake thought he felt her tremble. "You're a great k-kisser," she stuttered.

"It takes two." He winked at her.

The driver pulled into Brianna's apartment parking lot. "I got it," Jake informed the driver. He grabbed the bags and some of the stuffed animals and followed Brianna and her huge, fluffy white dog to the front door.

"Where do you want these?" he asked.

She switched on the lights. "You can put everything over there." She placed her white dog on the sofa. "You're so cute."

"Now that I won the dog, can we forget about a real dog?" he asked as he stood by the coffee table.

"You're not getting off that easy."

"That's what I thought."

They went back to the office so Brianna could pick up her car. "Call me when you get home," he told her after she got in her car.

"I'll think about it."

He watched Brianna pull away before rolling up the window. Once on the highway, he dialed Trent's number. "Can you talk?"

"What's up, man?"

"I just spent the day with Brianna, and I don't know how I'm going to survive a whole year with her."

"That bad? Well, I'm sure you'll think of something."

"Actually, we had a good time. After lunch, we went to Six Flags, hung out, kissed, and now she's going her way, and I'm going mine."

"Back up. Did you say kiss?"

"Normally, I don't kiss and tell, but, man, there

is something about this woman that is driving me crazy. One minute she's giving me plenty of attitude, and the next thing I know, she's flirting with me."

"You could be imagining it."

"I'm telling you, she's playing with me on purpose."

"Then stop playing her game. Keep her at arm's length. Go back to your original game plan."

"We ran into Samantha, too, so you know I was sweating."

"Man, you act like this is a real engagement."

"You're right. I'm tripping. Look, I'll talk to you later."

By the time Jake ended the call with Trent, the driver had dropped him off at home. He was going to his car to retrieve a book when his cell phone rang. "Glad you called."

"I started not to," Brianna said on the other end.

"Do you miss me?"

"Like a wart."

Jake laughed. "I take it you had a pimples problem when you were a teenager."

"Some folks should mind their business."

He could hear the laughter in her voice. He leaned on his car when he saw Samantha rush into the driveway, narrowly missing his car. "I'm just getting home, so I'll call you back," he said hastily.

He hung up with Brianna at the same time Samantha hopped out of her car and headed his way.

"Sam, what is your problem?"

"You. You think you can flaunt that woman in my face, and I wouldn't say anything."

"I thought we were cool. You said you understood."

"Coward." She stumbled and fell into his chest.

Jake didn't want to make a scene. Although the distance between the houses in his enclave wasn't close, if she got any louder, his neighbors would be able to hear her, and he didn't want a scene. He smelled the alcohol rising from her pores. "You've been drinking. Why don't you come in until you sober up?"

"I'm not going anywhere. I just came over here to give you a piece of my mind," she slurred.

"I don't think it's safe for you to drive, so why don't I call you a cab?"

She leaned harder on him. "Why don't you take me home? Come on, big boy." She reached for his crotch. He jumped back.

"Come inside. I'm calling you a cab."

This time she didn't resist and followed him inside. He called a cab while trying to fight her off. "You know, most men would be glad to have me, but you, you put me down for that fat heifer."

"I'd appreciate it if you didn't talk about Brianna like that."

"Why not me? Am I not good enough to marry?"

"Samantha, you and I would never work out, and you know it."

She stumbled over to him. "We could. You just never gave us a chance."

"You have a man, remember?"

"Forget him. It's you I've always wanted."

"This is not you. Pull yourself together."

Samantha went from begging to being outraged and then crying all in the span of five minutes. Jake did what he could to appease her until the cab showed up twenty minutes later. He gave the cab driver a hundred-dollar bill to make sure she got home and inside her place.

"You're going to wish you chose me. She'll never love you," she yelled as she got into the backseat of the cab.

As soon as they were gone, he called a tow truck and had her car towed to her place. He didn't want anything else to do with Samantha. He hoped her latest outburst would be the last of her, but his gut told him she would seek him out again. When or where, he didn't know.

Chapter 12

Brianna was too excited to go to sleep. She needed to talk to someone about Jake, or else she would be up all night. She normally would have called Bridget, but she didn't feel like hearing a lecture. Some of her friends were probably upset with her, because ever since her dad had died and she'd set out to get revenge, she had neglected to keep in contact with them. Besides an occasional e-mail, she barely talked to the friends she had grown up with.

Tosha was the only one she talked to on a regular basis. She dialed Tosha's number. Tosha picked up on the first ring. Before she could lose her nerve, Brianna blurted, "I have some news I want to share with you, but you can't tell anyone else. Promise me."

"Whew. Slow down, girl." Brianna could hear Tosha's television. "What's going on?"

"I took your advice, and I've been spending time with Jake. I mean, Jacob."

"Good. You deserve to be happy."

"There's more."

Tosha screamed, causing Brianna to remove the phone from her ear. "You did it! Was it good?"

"No, we haven't done it yet. But I can say he is a good kisser."

"You go, girl. Don't forget about me when you move to the big floor."

"I'm not going anywhere. Just because we're dating doesn't mean I'm getting a promotion."

"That's right. You left early. We got a memo letting us know you were being promoted to supervisor."

"Say what?"

"Your current supervisor shared the news. She didn't hesitate to let us know you were having an extended meeting with the CEO. If I were you, I would watch my back around her."

"Duly noted. Let me log in to check my e-mail. Shoot, I left my laptop at work."

"Must have been some meeting," said Tosha.

"Actually, between you and me, after lunch we went to Six Flags."

"What? While I'm slaving away at work, you're out living it up."

"Come on now. I said Six Flags. That's nothing."

"Actually, that's sweet. I wish someone would whisk me away in the middle of the day and take me somewhere."

"Please. Men are always doing nice things for you. It's not their fault you don't appreciate them."

"If your brother would come around, I wouldn't have to keep messing with these busters," Tosha pointed out.

"You and Bradford are too much alike. It would never work."

"Whatever, my future sister-in-law."

"Girl, I didn't realize how late it was. I'll see you in the morning." Brianna hung up the phone.

Eight hours later, Brianna fought with the covers as she hit the snooze button several times before getting out of bed. She made it to the office a few hours earlier than normal, because she needed to catch up on some work.

She focused on the project plan in front of her. Time went by fast, and before long, people were walking by her desk, congratulating her on her promotion. She peeped around her cubicle. Her supervisor's door stood open. She had a few things to say to her and hoped she could maintain her professional composure while doing so.

Brianna knocked on the outside door. "Diane, do you mind if I talk to you for a minute?"

Diane placed her jacket on her coatrack. "No, come right on in."

Brianna walked in, closed the door, and waited for Diane to sit. "I heard the promotion went through, and I appreciate you submitting my name for the position."

"You're welcome. You work hard, and I believe hard work should be rewarded."

"I am concerned about one thing."

"Is it the money? I got you as much as I could for the position."

Brianna shook her head. "No. It's the fact that everyone in the department knew I had a meeting with Jake. I mean, with Mr. Banks."

"To be honest, I didn't think it was a big deal. People were looking for you to congratulate you, so I just told a few people you would be out for the rest of the day."

"That's fine." Brianna stood up.

"Is there something you're not telling me?" Diane asked.

"No. Everything is fine."

Diane opened her mouth to say something but didn't. Brianna exited her office and returned to her desk. The new arrangement of flowers made her smile. She hoped no one had seen the card. She knew they were from Jake, but she wasn't prepared to share that bit of information with anyone yet.

"I wish someone would send me flowers once a week," one of her coworkers said as she passed by, admiring Brianna's beautiful tulip arrangement.

Brianna found the card. *I enjoyed playing hooky with you yesterday. Let's meet for dinner. J.*

She dialed the cell phone number on the card. She got his voice mail. "Thanks for the flowers. I'm busy tonight, but I am available tomorrow night," she said, leaving a message.

"Ask him if he has a brother," Tosha said, sneaking up behind her. "Girl, these are beautiful."

"Aren't they?"

"He's romantic, too."

"Shhh. Lower your voice," Brianna ordered.

"Girl, these folks don't know who I'm talking about."

"I don't need them all in my business, either."

"Tell your man to stop sending you flowers then."

Brianna put her headphones up to Tosha's ear so she could hear Jill Scott sing "Hate on Me." She sang some of the lyrics.

Tosha turned Brianna's MP3 player off and

handed the headphones back to her. "Come on. I'm hungry."

Brianna and Tosha ate lunch in the building's cafeteria. They spent the time gossiping about what was going on in their department. Brianna put a magazine up in front of her. "Don't turn around. Jake's in here."

Tosha pulled the magazine down. "He's coming this way, so you might as well put it down."

Brianna started putting food wrappers on her tray. Jake reached the table before she could make her escape. "Hi, ladies. Do you mind if I join you?" he said.

Tosha responded, "Have a seat."

Brianna looked up. Tosha was grinning from ear to ear. "Hi," she said, barely above a whisper.

Tosha cleared her throat. "I need to make a call. Chat with you later, Bri. Bye, Mr. Banks."

"Call me Jake."

Brianna wanted to pop Tosha for leaving her alone with Jake. "I'm leaving, too."

He reached out for Brianna's hand. "Stay a few. I wanted to talk to you."

Brianna looked around to see if anyone had noticed his gesture. Her paranoid behavior would get the best of her if she didn't watch it. She glanced at her watch. "I have a conference call in twenty minutes."

"I'm counting down the hours until our date tomorrow night."

Brianna blushed. She wasn't supposed to feel these types of emotions; falling in love with Jake made her giddy. If only they had met under different circumstances. "Jake. You don't have to do this. It's just us. We know it's all pretend."

"We're in this for a year, so we might as well make the best of it."

"True, but let's not go overboard."

"Admit it. You're attracted to me."

Brianna wanted to knock the smug look off Jake's face. Yes, of course, she found him attractive. She felt guilty admitting it to herself, so she refused to admit it to him. "I plead the fifth."

"Run for now, but eventually, you'll have to stop running."

"I'm running late for a meeting, so I guess it won't be today." She left the table before Jake could respond.

CHAPTER 13

After lunch Jake called Brianna's cell phone and desk phone. She avoided all his calls. Her developing feelings for him made it hard for her to think rationally. Because of the last name Banks, she refused to give in to the feelings haunting her day and night. The internal battle she fought was causing her to lose sleep at night. Love and guilt were replacing the feelings associated with revenge.

At the end of the day, Brianna made it out of the office building without running into Jake. She saw his silver sports car parked in its normal spot. She stopped her car behind Jake's for a moment, but the trance broke when a driver behind her blew his horn.

Bridget had been avoiding her calls all day. Instead of going home, Brianna decided to pay her sister a visit. She didn't want the tension of her upcoming nuptials to hurt their relationship. She had to make Bridget understand her ulterior motive, although lately, she wasn't so sure of her motive.

Bridget's SUV blocked most of the driveway, so

Brianna parked her car on the street. She dialed the house number once more, but no one picked up. She hoped coming over wasn't a mistake. A few seconds later, she stood at the front door, ringing the doorbell.

Bridget yelled, "Who is it?" Brianna didn't respond, so Bridget opened the door. "Oh, it's you."

"We need to talk." Brianna didn't wait for an invitation. She walked past Bridget, into the hallway.

Bridget slammed the door shut. "Benedict Arnold, what do you want?"

Brianna ignored her comment. She made her way to the kitchen to get a drink, with Bridget right behind her, on her heels. She took out a cold soda can and sat at the kitchen table. She took small sips. Bridget seemed frustrated, but eventually, she sat down at the table.

"I can always count on you to have a cold Sprite," Brianna noted, then released a few ahs to indicate how much she liked the drink.

"You could have gone to a convenience store for a drink. What gives?" Bridget asked.

"If you would have returned my calls, I wouldn't be sitting here."

"I'm pregnant, and I can't deal with too much stress, and that includes your mess."

Brianna reached for her younger sister's hand. "I'm not trying to stress you out. Give me five minutes and let me explain."

Bridget leaned back, with her arms folded, and rolled her eyes, a trait Brianna had also inherited.

"I'm not supposed to tell anyone, but if I go along with this, Jake has to pay me five million dollars. I plan on splitting it with you and Bradford."

"This doesn't make sense. So now you're a wife for hire?"

"No, nothing like that. As you know, Jack Banks recently died. Well, Jake's eccentric uncle has a clause in his will that states that Jake has to marry me, of all people, in order to get his inheritance."

"That's the silliest thing I've ever heard. There has to be more to it than that. I'll get Matt on it. Have you seen a copy of the will?"

"He showed me a portion of it."

"I don't like the idea of you sleeping with the enemy."

"Technically, it was Jake's uncle who turned down Dad, not Jake."

"He's a Banks, isn't he?"

"Yes," Brianna responded.

"Daddy used to say, 'The apple don't fall too far from the tree,' so Jake's not to be trusted."

"I never said I trusted him."

"Bri, you've done some crazy things, but this one here . . . Girl, I swear you're certified crazy."

"I'm doing what I have to do."

"Sweetie, you need to let it go. Dad's gone. We can't bring him back. Let it go. Put in some job applications elsewhere, and forget about Jacob Banks."

"Bridget, you just don't understand."

Brianna felt as if she was ten years old and was listening to her mother, and not her younger sister, reprimand her. Bridget went on and on about why marrying Jake wasn't a good idea. "You can't open up the *Dallas Morning News* without seeing him in the society pages. Can you handle being in the limelight? Your life will become an open book. Did you forget you're one of his employees?"

"Yes. No. I know how to deal with meddlesome reporters."

"But why even put yourself through it? I knew you going to work there was a bad idea."

Before Brianna could respond, Matt walked in the room. "There's my favorite girl." He walked over and kissed Bridget.

Brianna cleared her throat. "Excuse me. Can you two wait until I leave?"

Matt threw his hand up and waved. "Oh hi, Bri. Didn't see you sitting there."

Brianna cringed. "You're so full of it."

"Awe, sister-in-law." Matt walked over to where Brianna was sitting and bent down to hug her. "Better now?" he asked.

Brianna pouted. "Maybe."

"Hey, get your own. He's mine," Bridget said, smiling for the first time since Brianna stopped by.

Matt retrieved a bottle of water from the refrigerator. "Glad to see you two talking again. If you hadn't come over today, I would have called you myself."

Bridget looked at Matt as if she wanted to throw a dagger at him. "You talk too much."

"Baby, you just had me worried," Matt said as he pulled a chair near Bridget and sat down. He placed his arm around her shoulders.

"All is well now," Bridget assured him.

Brianna watched the two of them. The love between the two was what she wanted to experience. She wondered if she ever would. A lone tear slid down her cheek.

Bridget reached up and wiped Brianna's cheek. "Why don't you stay for dinner?" she asked. "I'm sure Matt doesn't mind." She looked at Matt, who didn't say anything.

"I am tired of fast food," Brianna admitted.

"It's settled. Matt's going to grill a few steaks, and I'll make some side items."

"Sounds good to me," Matt said as he stood up and kissed Bridget on the forehead.

Less than two hours later, they were enjoying a hearty meal. Bridget told Matt about Brianna's plans.

"Bri, this isn't the wisest thing you've done," Matt concluded.

"B-but . . . ," Brianna stuttered.

"I told you all before that trying to get revenge isn't worth it. Have you thought about all the people who might lose their jobs because of your plans?" Matt asked.

Brianna hadn't thought about it. Matt's question was valid, although she didn't admit it. "For now, I'm going along with the plan. I'll get the money and let the chips fall where they may."

CHAPTER 14

"Joan, thank you so much for setting the party up," Jake said.

Joan handed him a sheet of paper with the details of the party listed. "Happy engagement," she said before leaving him alone with his thoughts.

The first installment Jake received from his uncle's estate was enough to put Banks Telecom back in the black. Jake had to cut back in certain areas, but he was no longer hurting financially. He would be able to save his company and continue to live the lifestyle he had gotten accustomed to living. According to the will, he would receive the rest of the installments in phases, the bulk of it after he and Brianna remained married for a year.

He called Brianna on her cell phone. No answer. Where could she be? She had been avoiding him since lunch the day before. As a project manager, she was required to update her schedule in an online database that he had access to. He logged online to check her schedule and found that there weren't any meetings set up, so he concluded she was purposely avoiding his phone calls. She could avoid him at work, but he would be stopping by her place later, so he hoped she didn't plan on standing him up.

Jake spent about an hour at home preparing for his date with Brianna. Then glided through traffic in his sleek Jaguar. Holding a small bouquet of red roses, he knocked on Brianna's front door. He waited and waited. No one answered. Feeling dejected, he turned to walk away.

"I almost let you stay out here," Brianna said as she pulled the door open.

Her floral scent escaped out the door and attacked his senses before he heard her voice. He turned around. She stood there, fully dressed in an emerald green knee-length dress that accented her hips. His eyes glided from her hips to her face. Her dimples hypnotized him for a few seconds. "These are for you," he said as he handed her the roses.

Brianna sniffed them. "Thanks. Come on in." She pushed the door open.

Jake walked past Brianna and into her apartment. Silence loomed between them. Brianna exited the living room. Jake, feeling awkward, took a seat on her elegant sofa. While waiting for her to return, he picked up a women's magazine on her coffee table and flipped through it.

"I never would have thought the manly Mr. Banks read women's magazines," Brianna teased. She sat on the other end of the sofa.

"You got jokes." He laughed and placed the magazine back on the coffee table with the rest of the magazines.

"I owe you an apology."

He blinked his eyes a few times. "Don't wake me up if I'm dreaming."

"I did plan to stand you up tonight but realized I can't keep avoiding you if we are to pull off this charade."

"My ego thanks you."

She shook her head. "Men and their egos."

"I admit I don't like rejection."

She stood up. "Dear, you're not getting everything you want from me, so you might as well get used to it."

Two hours later, they were enjoying each other's company over a meal of enchiladas and burritos after attending a Mothers Against Drunk Driving charity event. After watching the videos at the event, he had needed something to cheer him up. He felt himself mesmerized by Brianna. Her laughter was contagious.

"You should laugh more," he stated.

"Keep me smiling," she teased.

"I have plenty of ways to do that, so test me." He took a bite out of his burrito. Some of the juices fell on his shirt.

Before he could react, Brianna had dipped her napkin in her water and was attempting to remove the stain. He hated to tell her it would only make it worse. Her close proximity made his heart skip a beat.

"You're such a big baby," she commented.

"You bring it out in me."

"Looks like you'll be taking this to the cleaners, because I can't get the stain out."

"Thanks for trying."

"No problem." She scooted her chair back.

"I wanted to discuss our engagement party." He reached into his pocket and unfolded a sheet of paper and handed it to her.

She reviewed it. "The Hilton Anatole. That's a nice place to have it."

"Joan needs your list of people by tomorrow, if you can have it."

"I can do that. There's only a few people I want to invite."

"I have something else for you, too." He reached into his pocket and pulled out an envelope. "This is yours."

Brianna opened up the envelope. She held up the platinum credit card with her name written on the front of it. "What's my limit?"

"There's no limit."

"Get out of here. Now you know better than telling a woman she has no limit on a credit card." She winked.

"I trust you won't go overboard."

"But you don't know that."

"You're always within budget on your projects."

"That's business. You're talking about me having access to anything I want without having to worry about a limit." She closed her eyes and opened them back up. "This is better than an orgasm." She shivered.

"If I had known I would get this type of reaction, I would have given you a card last week."

Brianna placed the card back in the envelope before putting it in her purse. "I'm going to have fun with this. First thing I'm getting is a new outfit. I need to find me something to wear to our engagement party. We should coordinate our colors."

"I had planned on wearing a gray suit. Nothing too fancy, but debonair."

"I'll find me a smoky gray dress that'll knock your socks off."

He sipped his drink. "You'll look good in whatever you wear."

She smiled and looked away. After a moment, she looked at him. "This seems real."

He reached over the table and touched her hand. "It is real. We can have many more nights like this."

She stared into his eyes. He sensed she was feeling the same thing he felt, a desire that went beyond the physical. They connected in more ways than one. He wanted to explore the feelings she stirred in him, but he didn't want to get hurt. Would his fantasizing become a reality? He hoped to find out soon.

CHAPTER 15

The next two weeks went by in a blur. She spent a lot of time trying to cover her tracks so the number fudging on a few projects couldn't be traced back to her. Although the rumor mill had her seeing Jake, the rumormongers were not aware that at the party they had been invited to, she and Jake would announce their upcoming nuptials.

Her time was also limited because Jake had insisted they get together a few more times so they could learn more about each other. She wasn't too thrilled about it but knew if they were going to pull it off, they needed to sound knowledgeable about each other when talking to others.

A few days before the event, he surprised her with a candlelight dinner at his house. She didn't want to admit it to him, but she loved his mini-mansion. The house seemed too big for two people, let alone one person. Moving in with him would be one of the few perks she enjoyed. It was big enough for them each to have their own suite.

As they stood in the foyer, Brianna fantasized

about her life in the Banks mansion. She felt guilty for getting caught up in the excitement. Jake snapped her out of her fantasy. "Do you think it would hurt you to show a little more enthusiasm?" he asked. "We are supposed to be getting married."

"What would you like me to do? I promise to smile and pretend that I'm overjoyed," she said sarcastically, while rolling her eyes.

"Follow me." He reached for her hand.

She took his hand and followed him into a room beautifully decorated with roses of various colors. "All of this for me?" she asked. She let go of his hand and walked over to get a closer view and a sniff of the flowers.

"Are these enough flowers for you?"

"Beautiful. Okay, you get a few brownie points for this move."

"Wow. I finally did something right." Jake clapped.

"You're not too bad." Brianna hated to admit that Jake would make a good boyfriend. A part of her wished the whole ordeal was real.

"How about a toast?" He walked to the bar and came back with a bottle of Moët and two flutes.

They sat down on the soft leather couch. She waited for him to pour his glass, and then they toasted. "To a new of our lives," she said as they clinked glasses. They both took a sip of their drink.

Jake placed his glass down on the table, then picked up one of the roses and handed it to Brianna. "To my future wife."

She sniffed the rose. Something sparkling caught her eye. She put her drink down and used her free hand to remove the ring lodged in between the rose petals. She held it up and inspected it. "This is big."

"Brianna, would you do me the honor and accept this ring as a symbol of our commitment to one another?" Jake took the ring from Brianna's hand and placed it on her finger. "It looks beautiful." His eyes seemed to twinkle as he said, "Just like you."

Brianna cleared her throat. "Sure. I mean, we have to look the part, don't we?" She moved her hand away. Brianna hadn't expected Jake to act romantic. She sure hadn't expected the gorgeous ring. She'd known he would get her something, but this ring was huge.

She stood up and pretended to view the other flowers. It was only a ploy to escape Jake's close scrutiny. She didn't want him to see her vulnerability. If he touched her, she would lose her reserve and they would end up in bed and it would mess up her whole world. She had to get away and now.

"Jake. The ring. I love it, but it's time that you take me home."

"It's still early. What's the big rush?"

"It's ten o'clock. Some of us have to work."

"I thought you were taking Friday off."

She was. Now she had to come up with another excuse. "I have a full day of pampering, and I need my beauty rest."

He stood up and reached for her. She jumped back, almost knocking over a vase. He caught her just in time. Their eyes locked. Jake said, "I'll take you home."

The ride home seemed long. Neither one said much to the other. Jake refused to let her walk up to her apartment by herself. She didn't want to argue, so she walked ahead of him, with him close behind.

Brianna unlocked her door, then held up her hand. "Thanks again for the beautiful ring."

Jake took her hand and kissed it, sending chills through her body. "This is only the beginning. Let's ride with the feeling."

She jerked her hand away. "I'll see you on Saturday night."

"I'll be by to pick you up around six."

"Until then." Brianna surprised both of them when she kissed Jake on the lips.

CHAPTER 16

The usual Friday night crowd at the Opal, a hot Dallas night spot, seemed to have doubled. Jake said "Excuse me" many times before making it to the table Trent had reserved. He wasn't surprised to see a couple of beautiful women hanging off Trent's arms when he approached.

Trent stood up and gave him dap. "This here is my man Jake. Jake, this is. . . . Forgive me, ladies."

"Cassie," the one with long brown tresses said, extending her hand.

The blond-haired one brushed Cassie's hand away and said, "And I'm Mindy."

"Nice meeting you both," replied Jake. He removed his jacket and placed it around the chair before taking a seat.

Trent said, "Jake's about to get married."

"The good ones are always taken," Mindy said as she pushed her chair closer to Jake. "But maybe we could have a little fun before you take the plunge."

Jake moved his chair back some. "I'll have to pass."

"Darn." Mindy stood up. "Cassie, I'll catch you later. I have some more mingling to do."

Cassie said, "Don't pay her any attention. She just broke up with her man, and she's looking to get laid."

Jake looked at Trent. Trent shrugged his shoulders, then he motioned for the waitress. She rushed over. "Give my man here anything he wants, and put it on my tab."

Jake ordered his usual Heineken and sat back and observed Trent and Cassie's public display of affection. Cassie's voluptuous assets were enough to make any man drool, and he bet Trent hadn't taken the time to find out what else she had to offer other than a good time. He found himself thinking about Brianna, about the way she licked her lips and the way she tilted her head right before letting out a hearty laugh. And her dimples. He wanted to dive into them. The twinkle in her eyes, which alerted him she was teasing him.

"Man, isn't she a cutie?" said Trent.

Jake wasn't aware Cassie had left. His mind was filled with thoughts of Brianna. His eyes followed Trent's gaze. "She's all right."

"Man, you know she's a dime piece."

"I got it bad, and I don't know what to do."

"You haven't hit it yet?"

"I don't kiss and tell. You know that."

"I sure would like to kiss that and would tell the world." Trent pointed in the direction of the door.

Jake turned around. "Man, that's my girl. I mean Brianna."

Brianna, who was accompanied by Tosha, wore a black minidress that clung to each one of her curves accenting her ample breasts. The four-inch black leather boots made her look even sexier.

"No wonder she got you swearing off other women." Trent held up his bottle of beer. "You the man."

"She didn't mention going out tonight."

"Whose the woman with her?"

"She's one of my employees."

Before Jake could tell him more, Cassie returned to the table. She plopped down in Trent's lap. "Miss me?"

"Of course," said Trent.

"Three's a crowd. I'm about to go mingle," Jake told them.

Jake made his way through the crowd. Brianna and Tosha were no longer in sight. He stood by the door and scanned the room. He spotted Brianna at one of the bars and walked over. "Hi, baby," he said, loud enough for the man trying to push up on Brianna to hear. He wrapped his arms around her and kissed her on the cheek.

"This is?" the other man asked.

Before Brianna could respond, Jake said, "Her man." He extended his hand.

The guy shook it. "I guess I'll be moving along."

"Yes, you do that," Jake said as he possessively put his arm around Brianna's shoulders.

Brianna laughed. "Jealous, are we?"

"It's not funny."

She pulled him closer. "Lighten up. You're taking this fiancé thing too seriously."

"Where's your ring, by the way?"

"I didn't feel like explaining anything to Tosha yet, so it's at home."

Tosha walked up to the bar. "Hi, boss."

"You can call me Jake." He shook her hand. "What are you ladies drinking?"

"Virgin daiquiri for me," Brianna said, taking a sip of the drink she held in her hand.

Tosha said, "Long Island iced tea. I've had a hell of a week. I need something a little stronger."

Jake pulled out a hundred-dollar bill and handed it to Tosha. "Drink up. Now let me steal your friend away."

"She's yours," said Tosha.

"Traitor," Brianna yelled.

Tosha took Brianna's drink and pulled her out of her chair. "Dance with the man."

Brianna looked at the two of them. "You both leave me no choice."

As if on cue, the music slowed down. One of his favorite Luther slow jams blasted through the room. He pulled Brianna closer to him. She relaxed and laid her head on his chest as they moved to the beat of the music.

Inhaling the fresh floral scent of her hair, he whispered, "I'm so glad you're mine."

"If only for one year," she responded as if her words were lyrics to the song.

He grabbed her hand and led her off the dance floor after the deejay sped it up with one of the latest hot dance songs. Trent and Cassie were no longer at their reserved table, so he pulled out a chair. Brianna sat down, exposing more of her legs as her dress crept up.

Jake hoped Brianna couldn't see the outline of his pants. He shifted in his chair until he got comfortable. He hated to admit it, but his attraction to Brianna went deeper than lust. An internal tug-of-war between lust and love made it hard for him to ignore what his heart felt.

CHAPTER 17

Brianna thought her night out on the town with Tosha would be interesting, but she hadn't expected to run into Jake. The more she was around him, the more she found herself being swept up in his make-believe world. Their first slow dance was to one of her favorite Luther songs. Now here they sat, next to each other, in a crowded club, but to her, it was as if they were the only two in the building.

A man and a woman sat down at their table. The man extended his hand to Brianna. "I'm Jake's best friend. Trent."

The woman didn't act too friendly. Brianna could barely hear her say "Cassie."

Jake said, "Trent and I were hanging out before the big party."

Brianna listened as Jake and Trent went back and forth. Trent reminded her of Tosha, whom she hadn't been able to locate since being thrust onto the dance floor with Jake.

"So you're the fiancée?" Cassie asked.

"Yes, and you're Trent's wife? Girlfriend?" replied Brianna.

"Neither right now, but I'm working on it." Cassie smiled and turned her attention back toward Trent.

Jake cleared his throat. "Look at the time. Trent, I'll see you tomorrow. Dear, you want to follow me?"

Brianna immediately saw through Cassie. Women like her had no problems using their assets to get what they wanted. She had met many women like Cassie. Some had been the cause of her relationships ending prematurely. Cassie reminded her of the woman she had caught Byron with. She hoped Trent was smart enough to see through her act.

Jake touched Brianna on the arm. "You go right ahead. I'm waiting on Tosha," she told him.

"I'll help you look for her," Jake said. He stood up and helped move her chair.

She gave in to his demands. "Nice meeting you, Trent."

Trent waved at her.

"You know she's only after his money," Brianna said as soon as they walked away.

"You don't have to worry about him. Trent's only after the booty."

"That figures," she said as she hit him playfully on the shoulder.

They walked through the crowd. Liquid splashed and hit her minidress. She moved back. "Darn it." She attempted to wipe her minidress.

"If it isn't the tramp and her boss," Charles slurred in his drunken state.

Jake jumped in front of Brianna, blocking her from Charles. "Man, I think you better chill."

"Or what? Pay me off." Charles stumbled forward.

Brianna tried to pull Jake away, but he wouldn't budge. They stood at a standstill. Finally, Jake said, "Bri. Come on."

She heard Charles yell obscenities as they walked away. She tried her best to ignore him. Tosha walked toward them as they made their way to one of the bars. "I saw what just happened," she said as she leaned close to Brianna.

"Girl, I don't know what I ever saw in him, with his drunk behind," Brianna whispered.

"If you're ready to go, I can leave and take you home," Tosha replied.

Jake intervened. "I can take her home."

"You sure? Is that okay with you?" Tosha asked, looking at Brianna.

"Stay. I'll ride with Jake."

"I was hoping you'd say that. See the tall cutie over there. He might be the one," Tosha proclaimed.

Brianna laughed. "Girl, every man you meet might be the one."

They hugged each other and said their good-byes. Brianna's night out on the town didn't end the way she had expected, but she did get to take home her own tall cutie. She grabbed Jake's hand and led him outside. They walked hand in hand to his SUV.

"So how long have you and Trent been friends?" she asked.

"Since as long as I can remember. He's like the brother I never had."

"Does he know about me? About us?"

By now Jake had hit the highway that led toward her place. "He knows about us."

"Everything?"

"Just about."

For the most part, Brianna really didn't care what people thought, but for some reason, it bothered her that Jake's friend knew most of the details of their arrangement. She reached over and turned up the volume of the stereo.

Jake turned the volume down. "I thought we had a nice time tonight. What's wrong?"

"Nothing."

"Yes, there is. Are you hurting because of Charles?"

Brianna laughed. "Please. Charles can kiss my behind."

"Then what is it?"

"Just take me home," she snapped. She turned her head away.

He turned the music back up. He didn't try to talk to her again until they reached her apartment. He opened her car door and followed her to the stairway. "I'll say my good night here. I don't want to fight with you."

"You're welcome to come up."

"I'll pass."

"Suit yourself." She felt disappointed, but she didn't blame him. She had snapped at him, but it wasn't his fault she was hurting. She desired love—real love—and knowing she was going into a loveless marriage hurt.

Brianna flipped the lights on in her apartment. It was late, but she wasn't sleepy. The need for male companionship overrode her need for revenge. She regretted that Jake hadn't accepted her invitation. A knock on the door startled her.

Maybe Jake had changed his mind. She peeped through the peephole and was disappointed to see it wasn't Jake.

"Charles, what do you want?" she called from behind the door.

"Let me in so we can talk."

"I'm all talked out."

"I'm sorry about what happened at the club."

"Whatever. Just go away."

"Bri, open this door now." He started beating on the door.

"You better hope one of my neighbors doesn't call the cops on you," she warned.

"Either you open the door or I'm camping out."

Charles's behavior wasn't normal. He was the one who had taken money to break up with her, but he acted as if she was the one who had broken up with him. She was not sure if he was serious or not, but she knew she wouldn't be able to sleep with him outside her door. She contemplated whether to call the police, then made a phone call.

"Jake, I need you," she blurted as soon as he answered his cell phone. She explained to him about Charles.

"I'm on my way. Don't open the door."

"You don't have to worry about that."

"Call the cops, and I'll be there as soon as I can. I'm turning around now."

She hung up with him and did as he had suggested. She went back to the door and peeped out the peephole. Charles's eye stared right back at her. She jumped.

He yelled, "You called your boyfriend, didn't you? Well, you know what? You're nothing but a paid whore. He paid for you, and he's getting his use out of you."

"So that makes you my john, since you took the money, now doesn't it?"

His sinister laugh caused her to back away from the door. "Baby girl, you won't be happy with him. I'll give back all the money. Well, the money I haven't spent, and we can go back to the way things were."

"Get away from the door," an officer shouted.

Charles blurted out obscenities, and a scuffle occurred. Brianna felt a thump against her door. The next sound was that of an officer knocking on her door. "Ms. Mayfield, open up. It's the police."

She looked out her peephole and saw the badge he held up to it. She opened the door and found two police officers. One had Charles in handcuffs. Jake stood behind them. He brushed past them to reach her. "Officers, I'm her fiancé," he announced.

One of the officers looked to her to confirm this. "Yes, he's my fiancé," she said.

Charles said, "Fiancé? You've been cheating on me all this time?" He attempted to come at Brianna but was jerked back by the other officer.

"I'll need to get your statement," the officer said, while the other officer escorted Charles away.

Charles continued to yell out obscenities. Some of her neighbors now stood in their doorways, watching the entire scene. Brianna couldn't wait to move. She had never been so embarrassed. She welcomed the officer in. She didn't want to file charges against Charles; she just wanted him to leave her alone. Jake's arm around her shoulders during the questioning comforted her.

"Since one of your neighbors also reported

a disturbance, we can fine him for disturbing the peace. If he does anything else, here's my card." The officer handed her a card with all his information.

"Thank you, Officer Mandle," she replied.

"You two enjoy the rest of your night. Well, what's left of it, anyway."

"Thanks, Officer," Jake responded.

Jake locked the door behind the officer. He held his arms out, and Brianna closed her eyes and fell into his warm embrace. Jake no longer seemed like the enemy. Brianna was seeing him in a whole new light.

CHAPTER 18

Jake wanted to wring Charles's neck for frightening Brianna. The fact that she felt comfortable calling him about the situation said more than she could say with words. He held her in his arms and didn't want to let go.

"Do you need me to stay the night?" he asked.

"No, but I want to thank you for coming. It really means a lot." She seemed to retreat back into her shell.

"Call me Superman," he joked.

She removed herself from his embrace and looked at the clock. "It is late, so on second thought, why don't you stay?"

"This is my lucky night."

"Hold up. You're sleeping on the couch."

"I don't know. I did drive all the way over here. Can I at least get the bed?"

"We're two adults. You can sleep on one end, and I on the other. And before you get any ideas, you're keeping your clothes on."

"Can I at least take my socks off?" he asked as he followed her to her bedroom, which looked just as feminine as she was. The soft, bright colors seemed to reflect her jubilant personality.

"If your feet stink, you'll have to keep them on."

"I don't have stinky feet."

"I'll be the judge of that."

Brianna changed into a pair of maroon floral satin pajamas. She could have worn a flannel gown, and he still would have found her sexy. Tempted to release her ponytail, instead he used his hands to unbutton his shirt.

"What are you doing?" she yelled.

"I'm taking off this shirt. Don't worry. I got a T-shirt under here."

"I guess it's all right."

She sectioned off the bed with an extra blanket as he took off his shirt. He caught her watching him a few times. He smiled.

He got under the covers, with his head at the foot of the bed. "Good night, Brianna."

She mumbled, "Good night."

Although Brianna's bed was spacious, he felt uncomfortable. He turned in different directions and could not get comfortable. "Brianna, I'm not used to sleeping at the end of the bed. Can I come up there where you are?"

For a moment he thought she had fallen asleep. Then she growled, "If that means you'll stop moving around, come on."

He grabbed his pillow and moved to the head of the bed. "Now that's better."

She tugged on the bedspread. "Be quiet and go to sleep please."

"You sound tense. I know how to release some of the pressure."

Brianna reached behind her, grabbed her

pillow, and hit Jake upside the head with it. "Oh, you want a fight. You got one."

He couldn't believe it. Here he was, a thirty-six-year-old man, having a pillow fight, and it felt good. "I give up," he finally said as they both doubled over with laughter.

"I needed that stress release. The only thing that would have made it better is if I could have gone upside Charles's head," Brianna said.

"Anything else I can do to help?" he asked as he leaned on his elbow and looked into her eyes.

"Just hold me and go to sleep."

"Your wish is granted."

Brianna turned her back to him and snuggled close to him. He shifted his body so she wouldn't feel the erection developing due to her slight movement. Before long, they both were asleep.

The sun beaming through the curtains and Brianna removing his arm from around her woke Jake up. It took him a few minutes to realize where he was. "Bri? Baby, where are you going?"

"I have a day of pampering ahead of me. I can't stay in bed all day."

"What time is it?" He looked around for a clock but didn't see one.

"It's almost noon."

"Man, I can't recall the last time I slept this late."

"Me either. But, hey, you're welcome to wait around, but I'm about to go get in the shower."

"Maybe I can join you."

She stood up and threw a pillow at him. This time he ducked. "No such luck."

"You go bathe and I'll be here."

He went to her second bathroom and washed

up. He roamed through her refrigerator and found some breakfast items and cooked while waiting for her to get dressed. Since he had a few things to take care of himself, he utilized her microwave to do a quick meal.

He had just removed two slices of toast when she came in, dressed in a pair of blue jeans and a New Orleans Saints T-shirt.

"I didn't know you were handy in the kitchen," she said.

"There's a lot you don't know about me," he responded as he placed the bacon and eggs on two separate plates.

"Good job," she said as she poured two glasses of orange juice.

They chatted over what could now be considered brunch, because of the time.

"What's with the Saints shirt? You know you're in Cowboys country?"

"My brother played for the Saints until he hurt his knee," she said nonchalantly.

"Which position?"

"I think it was linebacker. Or was it running back? Shoot, I don't know. I'm not a football fan."

"You won't have to worry about me taking you to any games."

"Good, but if you get some tickets to a Mavericks game, you better hook me up."

"I can do better than that. I have a skybox."

"Cool. Then it's on."

Brianna enjoyed their back-and-forth bantering. Being in his arms the night before had stirred up emotions she had thought were long gone. The more time she spent around Jake, the more the desire to get revenge on him waned.

Maybe Bridget and Bradford were right. Maybe

she should give up her quest for revenge. If she did that, could she really move on? She could renege on the contract she had signed with Jake, but where would she hide? She had grown up in Dallas and had no plans of relocating. She knew Jake would hunt her down to make her live up to her end of the agreement. She would see this situation through. It might cost her—but how much was the million-dollar question.

CHAPTER 19

Brianna's rapid heartbeat seemed to overshadow all other sounds in the room. She paced back and forth, questioning her sanity for agreeing to go along with Jake's proposition. She checked her reflection in the mirror for the umpteenth time. Satisfied with what she saw staring back at her, she smiled. The smoky gray evening dress would match Jake's eyes perfectly. The hours at the beauty salon had been well spent. Her hair was pinned up, with a few cascading curls flowing down on the sides. The style accented her oval-shaped face and dimples, which were a family trait. The only thing left for Brianna to do was to remove her glasses and replace them with contacts.

Her cell phone beeped to indicate she had messages. Putting the phone on speaker, Brianna listened as her siblings pleaded with her to think about what she was doing one last time. She decided not to return their calls and hoped that they would show up and that they were on their best behavior if they did. Jake left a message to confirm he was on the way.

At the last minute, Brianna decided to call Tosha and warn her of the real purpose of the party. Tosha didn't answer her phone. "Oh well, she'll find out like everybody else," Brianna said aloud.

She retrieved the ring from her jewelry box. The two-carat princess-cut ring glistened as she placed it on her finger. Her mother and father had given her a pair of diamond earrings and a matching necklace when she graduated from college. She put those on as tears formed in her eyes.

"I'm not going to cry," she told herself as she used a tissue to wipe her eyes. Brianna missed her parents. It saddened her that her dad would have been disappointed in her decision to marry Jake, because he was a Banks. Her mother, on the other hand, would have told her to follow her heart. Her heart and mind were in constant turmoil over these new feelings for Jake.

A knock at the door made Brianna push her thoughts to the side. "Coming," she yelled. She peeped through the peephole out of habit. A man in a black uniform and hat was outside the door. "Who is it?" she asked.

"I'm your limousine driver. Mr. Banks asked me to get you," he responded.

"Give me a minute, and I'll be ready," she said as she opened the door.

Jake stood outside the white stretched limousine as she walked down the walkway. Brianna felt like she was on a red carpet as people in her apartment complex stared. "You look stunning," he said as he bent down to plant a kiss on her lips.

The driver opened the limousine door. She

gathered up her dress and entered, with Jake right behind her. The ride over to the Hilton Anatole ballroom was pleasant.

"I booked an executive suite to give us time to unwind while the guests arrive. At seven we'll make our grand entrance," Jake told her.

Brianna rubbed the palms of her hands together. "Everything's moving so fast."

Jake reached out and placed his hand on top of hers. "Relax. We can do this."

"From this day forward, everything is going to change."

"Change is good, right?"

She sighed. "That's what I hear."

Brianna had been to the hotel before for several events and a couple of dates, but the executive suite Jake had booked left her speechless. Everything she could have imagined wanting, he had made sure was there. He even had several extra pairs of hosiery just in case she needed to change.

She hadn't eaten anything since breakfast. Her stomach reminded her of the fact, especially after she saw several delectable trays of seafood. She made a straight beeline for the trays.

"These are delicious," she said in between bites.

"I recall that in one of our conversations, you mentioned your love of shrimp and crab cakes."

"I'll have to add some more brownie points to your score."

"When can I cash those in?"

"I'll let you know, but in the meantime, can you pass me another one of those stuffed shrimp?"

"Anything for you, dear." Jake placed a few of the stuffed shrimps on her plate. He held one in his hand and fed it to her.

"Mmm. Delicious." She licked her lips.

Jake focused on her mouth. She took one of her stuffed shrimps and fed him. He kissed her fingers.

"Are you nervous?" Brianna asked.

"Who me? Of course not." His eyes sparkled.

"You're lying," Brianna responded.

Jake placed his hand over his heart. "You see right through me."

Brianna laughed. "You're so full of it."

Brianna enjoyed their little cat and mouse game. The phone rang, interrupting them. Jake answered, and after hanging up, he said, "It's time. Most of our guests have arrived."

Brianna's nerves had her sweating, so she stopped in front of the mirror to make sure her makeup wasn't ruined.

"You look fine," he assured her.

She patted her forehead with a napkin and threw it in the trash, then retrieved her purse. "Okay. I'm ready."

They took an exclusive elevator reserved for executives up to the ballroom, where their party was in full swing. She could hear the music before they arrived. They were directed through a side entrance. She glanced around the curtain and was relieved to see Bridget, Matt, and Bradford standing near the front. She would focus on them when she made her entrance.

Jake whispered, "Ready?"

Brianna gave him the thumbs-up signal.

The music stopped, but the noise took longer to die down. Soon afterward, the guests quieted down enough for Jake to be heard. He spoke into the microphone. "Thank you all for coming tonight. I know for some of you, it was very short notice. I know everyone is curious about my big announcement."

Brianna heard a few people yell "Yes."

Jake went on. "I won't keep you in further suspense. Have you ever met someone, and you knew the person would have a lasting effect on your life? Well, that happened to me when I met this special woman. My life hasn't been the same since she walked into it. She's put a smile on my face, and as some folks would say, some pep in my step."

A few people laughed.

"For all you single ladies, I'm no longer on the market. I want you all to meet the future Mrs. Banks. That's right. I want you to meet my lovely fiancée."

Brianna was amazed at Jake's speech. She almost believed the words he had said herself. That was her cue to come out onstage. He extended his hand, and she walked to where he stood and took a hold of his hand. Mumbling could be heard throughout the room.

"Ladies and gentlemen, I introduce to you Brianna Mayfield, the future Mrs. Banks," said Jake.

Before she could react, her eyes were blinded by the flashing cameras. When her eyes adjusted, Brianna scanned the room. She could tell some of the people in attendance, mainly her coworkers, were in shock. Her eyes locked with Tosha's, and she waved. Her eyes locked with her ex-supervisor, and if looks could kill, she would be dead on the spot. She looked at her brother and sister. She couldn't tell what they were thinking. She would soon find out, because they were headed in her direction.

CHAPTER 20

"If I didn't love you, I wouldn't be here," Bridget whispered in Brianna's ear while giving her a hug.

Brianna responded, "Thank you. We'll talk later."

"Yes, we need to," Bridget said as she removed herself from Brianna's embrace and faced Jake.

Brianna said, "Jacob, this is my sister, Bridget."

"Call me Jake." Jake extended his hand. Bridget shook it, but reluctantly.

Matt shook Jake's hand. "I'm Matt, Bridget's husband."

Brianna continued to make the introductions. "This is my brother, Bradford, and . . ."

"Sierra," said the petite woman hanging on Bradford's arm.

"Nice to meet you all," said Jake. Bradford didn't refuse to shake Jake's hand, but he didn't have much to say either until Jake said, "The Saints need you right now, man."

Bradford responded, "Don't count them out yet. Reggie Bush is a force to be reckoned with."

After talking about football for a few minutes, Jake got a server's attention, and each person took a flute off the server's tray, except for Bridget. Jake looked in Brianna's eyes and said, "Here's to a wonderful life with my future wife."

Bridget rolled her eyes. Matt squeezed her hand and drank his champagne faster than he normally would have. Brianna gulped hers down fast. Other folks vied for Jake's attention.

"Jake, I'll be right back," Brianna said as her family moved to the background to allow others to get closer.

"Don't leave me to face all these people by myself," he pleaded.

She stayed by his side but kept an eye on Bridget.

"Brianna, you don't know how surprised I am," Diane said as she made her way through the receiving line.

"It all happened so fast," Brianna responded. She barely looked at Diane. She tried to keep Bridget in her view. She could tell Bridget still wasn't too happy about her plans.

"No wonder I didn't get any opposition to your promotion," Diane snapped and walked away.

That got Brianna's attention. "No, that heifer didn't," she said, unaware she had spoken out loud.

"My boy. Congratulations," Trent said, giving Jake a hug. "And my new sister-in-law."

Brianna hugged him, although her mind was on Diane. She would have to set her straight.

"If you change your mind, I'm still available," Trent joked.

Brianna plastered on a smile. "I don't know. You might be too much for me to handle."

"You're probably right," agreed Trent.

They all laughed.

Brianna commented, "Where's your date? What is her name? Cassie."

"She didn't work out. Too clingy," Trent confessed.

"Or too dingy, if you ask me," quipped Brianna.

Trent hit Jake on the back. "I like her. She's definitely a keeper."

Tosha made her way up to the front of the line. "Congratulations." She hugged Brianna and whispered in her ear, "I got a bone to pick with you."

"I called to tell you, but you never answered your phone," said Brianna in her defense.

"No excuse. You had plenty of time to tell me," Tosha scolded.

They turned in Trent's direction after he cleared his throat a few times. Brianna introduced them. "Tosha, this is Jake's best friend, Trent."

Trent picked up her hand and kissed the back of it. Bridget actually saw Tosha blush. Tosha never blushed. "You two must be the most beautiful women in the place tonight," Trent proclaimed.

"You're probably right," Tosha responded.

Jake looked at Brianna, and they laughed. Then he said, "I hate to break up this love fest, but there are folks behind you."

Trent said, "Oh, my bad. Tosha, let's move over here. I would really like to talk to you more."

"You're forgiven," Tosha said to Brianna before moving.

Joan walked up and hugged Brianna. "Take care of Jake. He might not admit it, but he needs you."

"But . . ." Brianna started to say something else but stopped herself.

"You did a great job," Jake said as he hugged Joan.

Brianna and Jake spent the next thirty minutes shaking hands with business associates and friends and accepting congratulatory comments. Brianna's emotions were on a roller-coaster ride. She was happy that most folks seemed to be sincere, but she couldn't help being concerned about Bridget. Would her decision to move forward with marrying Jake create a wedge between them? When the crowd thinned out, Brianna made her escape to look for Bridget.

"She's in the bathroom," Matt informed her. "Since she got pregnant, morning sickness seems to hit at the oddest times."

Brianna made a beeline for the bathroom. She paused before going around a corner when she overheard a female voice say, "No wonder she got the promotion. Sleeping with the boss is a guarantee."

Another woman said, "The position was supposed to be mine. I ought to sue."

"If I were you, I would," the other one said, trying to encourage her.

Brianna stood and waited until they were out of hearing distance, and then she rushed into the bathroom. She forgot about the two ladies when she saw Bridget standing at the sink, wiping her face.

"You okay?"

"I am now. This morning sickness should be called all-day sickness, because the slightest thing can send my stomach into a frenzy."

"Maybe the doctor can give you something for it."

"Ha. And maybe I'll win the lottery. No. I have to ride this out."

"You're making me change my mind about having kids," Brianna said.

"I wish I could change your mind about marrying that man," Bridget snapped.

"Sis, we've been through this."

"It's not fair to you. You deserve better. You deserve what Matt and I have."

"I will have it. Just not right now."

"You need to let this quest for revenge go and move on with your life."

"I can't. Not now. I've come too far to stop now."

"It's never too late," Bridget assured her.

"But . . ." Brianna cut herself off as Diane came through the bathroom door.

Diane acknowledged her by saying "Brianna" before entering a stall.

"Who is that?" Bridget whispered.

"My ex-supervisor."

"What's going on?"

"Nothing. I just need to get something straight."

"You need me to stick around?" Bridget asked.

"No. I got this."

"You sure?"

"Positive."

Bridget looked away from the stall and glanced in the mirror and reapplied her lipstick. "Let me get back to Matt before he starts worrying."

"I'll be out in a minute."

Brianna waited for Diane to exit the stall.

Diane exited and bumped into her and jumped. "Ooh, you scared me."

Brianna didn't waste any time. "I don't appreciate the comment you made earlier. I got my promotion fair and square."

"I'm not saying you didn't work hard, but it's interesting that your promotion happened so fast."

"You're the one who recommended me. Did I come to you, asking for it? No."

"I know that and you know that, but you know others will be talking."

"They'll be talking only because you're adding fuel to the flames."

"Brianna, I've always liked you, but lately your demeanor has changed. Hearing you're engaged to the CEO makes me understand why."

Brianna moved closer to Diane. Diane moved back, bumping into the sink. "Let's get one thing clear. I've worked hard for my promotion, and if I hear you've said otherwise, you will have to answer to me."

Diane stuttered, "I . . . I haven't been saying anything."

Brianna's main focus had been on Diane. She hadn't realized other women had piled into the bathroom. A hush fell over the room. No one dared to say anything to her after watching the scene. Brianna stormed past them in search of Jake.

CHAPTER 21

Jake saw Brianna and could tell something was wrong from how quickly she walked. He stood up and moved her chair out. She plopped down and didn't say a word. He had hoped that rearranging their seating and having family sit at their table would make her happy. He watched her down the drink in her flute.

"Slow down. You need to eat something," he told her.

"I can take care of myself," she responded just a little too loudly.

He tried to remain calm. He rubbed her back with the palm of his hand. "I know that, but you've been downing those and haven't eaten much."

"I'm hungry." She picked up one of the strawberries on the tray in front of them.

As if on cue, the food was brought out, and everyone was served. The conversation over dinner was light.

The rest of the night was filled with conversation and congratulatory comments. Jake was tired. He felt as if he was running for political office the way he had smiled and laughed throughout the whole night. He also felt as if the engagement was more than a business deal. He hoped Brianna would soon feel the same way.

Brianna seemed like a walking time bomb. Earlier, she had appeared happy, but after returning to their hotel suite, she seemed aloof. He tried to get her to open up to him, but she snapped at him a few times, so he thought it was best to drop the subject.

They retreated to separate rooms. Jake changed into a pair of pajamas and waited to see if Brianna would return to his part of the suite so they could talk about the night's events. He wanted—no, he needed—to know how she felt. This thing between them was beyond sexual. Yes, his body desired to fill her body, but his soul desired to fill her heart. He waited, but she never returned from her room. He turned out the light and went to bed, with thoughts of Brianna invading his dreams.

The next morning Jake found himself taking a cold shower. The thought of Brianna in his hotel suite had him stiff as a board. His body needed some sexual release and soon. After taking a long shower, he dressed and went in search of Brianna.

Jake was surprised to find her sitting, with her legs crossed, on the sofa. He was even more surprised when she greeted him with a hug. "I take it you're feeling better this morning," he stated.

"About last night. I just needed some alone time."

He cleared his throat. "I understand. Are you

hungry? They have a nice brunch. I'll have them bring it up."

"It's already on the way. I heard you in the shower, so I decided to order. Hope that's all right."

"Of course. You're the future Mrs. Banks, so you might as well act like it."

She put down the magazine she was reading. "I did perform in a few school plays."

"You know what I mean."

Brianna had a serious look on her face. "Jake, how do you feel about me?"

Jake wasn't prepared to answer. "I like you well enough."

She curled her legs up under her. "That's not what I meant, and you know it."

"What I'm feeling is all new to me."

"We seem to have this tug-of-war going on. One moment we're having a nice talk, and then the next, it's like we're trying to one-up the other," Brianna confessed.

"I think it's more you than me."

Brianna picked up the pillow on the sofa and threw it at him. "Why did I think I could have a serious conversation with you?"

Someone knocked on the door, saving him from answering. It was a waiter delivering their room service brunch. The conversation resumed as soon as the waiter left.

"This looks good," Brianna said as she piled food onto her plate.

"It sure does," Jake responded, not once taking his eyes off her.

"If you're going to stare, you can at least answer my question."

"Which is?"

"Jake, I don't have time to play this little game of yours. I was trying to see where your head was, but it's obvious to me, you're not ready to talk about it."

"Let's just enjoy brunch, and we can talk later."

"As far as I'm concerned, the topic is closed." She dug into her pancakes. "Pass me the salt please."

Jake had originally planned to spend the whole day with Brianna, but she insisted on going home after they ate brunch. The limousine dropped her off first before driving him home. His voice mail on his home phone was filled with messages from women he had dated. Word had gotten out about his engagement due to an article and pictures in the Dallas paper. Some of the women congratulated him, while a few cursed him out. Trent had left him a message about Tosha.

"Please don't tell me you did what I think you did," he said as soon as Trent answered his phone.

"We were two consenting adults. So why you tripping?"

"Number one, because she's my fiancée's friend, and number two, because she's one of my employees, and I know how you like to love them and leave them."

"Tosha's a big girl. It's me you should be worried about." Trent laughed on the other end of the line.

"I have enough going on and don't need to be involved in your mess."

"I should be offended, but I'm not."

"I'll talk to you later. I have a busy week ahead, and I'm about to get me some rest."

"Tell that fine fiancée of yours I said hello."

"I will whenever I talk to her."

"You two seemed to be really in love, man. You had me fooled."

"I have a confession to make."

"You're not still kicking it with Samantha, are you?"

"No, bucket head. Shut up before I lose my nerve."

"What is it, man?"

"I think I'm really falling in love with Brianna, and I don't know what to do."

There was silence on the phone. Jake called out Trent's name several times.

Finally, Trent said, "I know this isn't the man who said there's not a woman alive who can capture his heart."

"I'm eating my words now because Brianna has got my nose wide open. Maybe Uncle Jack knew something I didn't know, and that's why he set this all up."

"So what are you going to do about it?"

"Nothing. She gave me the chance to tell her how I felt, but I clammed up."

"Talk to her. You two are getting married, so tell her."

"I can't believe I'm admitting this, but I'm afraid to."

"You are Jacob Banks, the CEO of his own company, a person who has made multimillion-dollar deals. So man up, and tell the woman how you feel. You might be surprised. From what I observed, I bet she feels the same way."

"Trent, you're right. I'm telling Brianna how I feel, and she will just have to deal with it."

CHAPTER 22

"Congratulations," one of Brianna's coworkers told her as she made her way to her new office.

Others congratulated her, too. Some were sincere; some were doing it only because they thought it was the customary thing to do.

When she entered her office, she found Jake sitting behind her desk, holding a bouquet of flowers. "Good morning."

She quickly closed her door. "What are you doing here?"

"The word is out now, so we don't have to tiptoe around each other."

Brianna placed her laptop on her desk and took the flowers from Jake's hand as he remained in her chair. "You act like we're really a couple."

"We are. At least to everyone else," he said before pulling her onto his lap.

She hit him on the chest. "What are you doing?"

"Something I've been wanting to do since last week."

Jake reached his hand behind her neck, and their lips locked, making Brianna melt. His tongue darted inside her mouth. She wanted to give in to her emotions, but she didn't want to get hurt. Falling in love with Jake was not part of the program. Not at all. She gathered her composure and pushed him away. Then she stood up and ran her hand over her skirt to get rid of the wrinkles.

"Let's not do this," she said.

Jake stood up and kissed her on the forehead. "I'll call you later."

Brianna stood watching him walk out. He left her door open. She slid behind her desk and inhaled Jake's masculine scent, mixed with the scents of the flowers. She refused to get caught up in emotions. She had work to do.

Brianna spent the morning reading over policies and procedures for her new position. Around lunchtime Tosha walked in, holding two bags from a local deli. "Since you're not answering your phone, I thought I would take a chance and find you here."

"I'm waiting on the IT guys to hook my phone up."

"No telling how long that'll be." Tosha closed her door before handing Brianna a bag.

"Thanks for the food. I let time get away from me."

"I figured you wouldn't want to go to the cafeteria."

Brianna removed a sandwich from the bag and a drink. "You've thought of everything."

"Yep." Tosha didn't retrieve her sandwich. She sat back and crossed her legs.

Brianna looked up after taking a few bites. "So what's up? You guys miss me?"

Tosha leaned forward. "Girl, you and Jake are

the talk of the town. Did you see the write-up in Sunday's paper?"

"I saw it. Don't know why it's such a big deal, but it was nice."

"Girl, you're taking one of Dallas's most eligible bachelors off the market. That's a big deal. And these heifers up here are hating on you big-time. I almost popped one in the mouth earlier for saying you got your new position because of your relationship with Mr. Banks."

"I appreciate you sticking up for me, but, girl, let them talk. I got this promotion because of my hard work in the boardroom, not the bedroom."

"I am upset with you, though," Tosha stated.

"How many times do I have to tell you? I tried to call you."

"This is what I don't get. Just a few weeks ago, you were contemplating whether or not to date him, and now you're getting married. This has to be the shortest courtship I've ever seen."

Brianna shrugged her shoulders. "What can I say? I told him if he wanted the goodies, the only way was for him to marry me." She held out her hand. "And the rest is history."

"I wouldn't have said no to it. Or to that, either." Tosha held up Brianna's hand, admiring her ring close up. "This baby is pretty."

Brianna tried to pull her hand away, but Tosha wouldn't let go. "My hand," Brianna said.

Tosha finally let her hand go. "Let me tell you about Trent. Girl, talk about working it. I think I'm in lust. He knew how to hit every last one of my spots."

"I can't believe you slept with him. You just met."

Tosha faked innocence. "I couldn't resist. I'm on the rebound."

Brianna sighed. "Don't get caught up. Just from the few times I've seen Trent, I can tell he is a handful. More so than Jake."

"You handle Jake, and let me worry about Trent. Trent's met his match. He might be a Mac Daddy, but I'm the queen of mac."

Brianna laughed. "That you are."

They spent the remainder of the time talking about the party and men. Finally, Tosha said, "Some of us don't have this luxury, so I better get back to work before Diane pitches a fit."

"She hasn't said anything, has she?" Brianna asked as she cleared off her desk.

"Not to me."

"If she does, make sure you tell me. I don't like how she stepped to me the other night."

"She's just jealous because her sorry husband is cheating on her and got them in a ton of debt."

"I'm not going to even ask you how you know all that."

Tosha looked away. "I can't help it if folks like to tell me things."

"Uh-huh. Well, you better go. I don't want to be accused of being a bad influence."

Brianna's first day in her new role didn't go as badly as she had thought it would. At the end of the day, she hummed as she walked to her car. She stopped in midstep when she saw Charles standing next to the driver's side of her car.

"I could get you for stalking," she snapped.

"I made a mistake," Charles stated.

"Yes, you did. It being coming here."

"I told you I would give back the money. I love you, Bri, and I'm sorry."

She looked him directly in the eyes. "I admit

what you did pissed me off, but I'm over it. Move on. I sure did."

"It's not going to work between you two. He doesn't love you like I do."

"I'm glad, because your love is for sale. Hopefully, his isn't." He continued to block her way.

"Move," she said. He didn't budge. She reached for her cell phone.

"I'm leaving. If you ever need anything, I want you to know I'm there," he said.

"Don't hold your breath," she muttered.

Charles stomped away.

CHAPTER 23

Jake had witnessed the whole scene. He walked up to Charles. "If I catch you anywhere near her again, you don't have to worry about the cops."

"I'm not trying to cause any trouble, okay. I just wanted to apologize to Bri for what happened," Charles explained.

"You could have done that over the phone or by e-mail," Jake growled.

Charles ignored him and walked away. Jake stood there and waited for him to get in his car and drive off. As soon as he did, Jake hopped in his car, pulled out of the parking garage, and dialed Brianna's cell phone number. "I just saw you talking to your ex. Are you okay?"

"I'm fine."

He listened as Brianna described their encounter. "You should have walked the other way as soon as you saw him."

"Look. I know how to handle Charles."

"You forgot about last week. What if he had had a weapon? How would you have protected yourself?"

"Jake, I'm so glad you care."

"You're the most difficult, stubborn woman I know."

"And you're the most egotistical male chauvinist I know."

Jake was fuming and had to calm down. He took a deep breath. "Bri, I care about you. You mean more to me than you think," he confessed.

"I'm a means to an end, so don't pretend otherwise."

"I'm not going to argue with you."

"We're having a mature conversation."

"Sometimes I want to just . . ." He paused as he slammed on his brakes. The car behind him didn't stop in time. His cell phone flew out of his hands, and his air bags deployed. He reached for the phone but blacked out.

When he woke up, he was in a hospital room at Presbyterian Hospital. Trent sat at the end of the hospital bed. Jake smiled when he saw Brianna sitting in the chair right next to him.

"Where am I?" he asked.

Brianna stood and made her way to his side. She held his hand and said, "You were in an accident. We were on the phone, and the next thing I heard was a crash."

Trent stood up and walked to the other side of the bed. "Yes. You had us worried, man. I freaked out when Joan called me."

Jake looked at Brianna. "Thank you for being here."

She squeezed his hand. "I'm trying to get you down the aisle. You can't bail out on me now."

He didn't want to get his hopes up, but by

showing up at the hospital, Brianna had acknowledged that she cared more than she let on, even
if she didn't want to admit it. He sat up but then
slid back down. His head throbbed from the
pain. "Where's the doctor? When can I get out of
here?"

Trent said, "Slow down, player. You have a con-
cussion. I'll go get the doctor to let him know
you're awake."

After Trent left the room, Jake asked, "How
did you find out?"

"I heard the crash, and when you didn't respond to me yelling into the phone, I hung up,
did a U-turn, and called nine-one-one. I figured
you weren't that far from the office."

"My Jag. Is it okay?"

"Your car's a little beat up, but don't worry
about that. At least you're going to be fine."

He rubbed the top of his head. "I don't know.
It hurts to sit up."

"Trent went to get the doctor, so I'll make sure
I tell him."

A dark-skinned foreign doctor walked in, with
Trent behind him. "Mr. Banks, I'm Dr. Razi."

Jake tried unsuccessfully to sit up again. "My
head hurts every time I sit up."

Brianna and Trent moved to the background
as the doctor examined him. "We need to run a
few tests. I'll have the nurse give you some medicine for the headache."

Jake wouldn't admit to anyone he was scared
of doctors. He recalled going to the hospital with
his uncle Jack. And he would never forget the
last time he saw his father alive. The memory of
his father in a hospital bed also brought back
memories of his parents' fatal car accident. His

mom had died upon impact, but his dad, he had fought. It wasn't until he had seen Jake that he seemed to be at peace and died, leaving Jake in the care of his uncle.

Tears flowed from Jake's eyes as he recalled the childhood memory. Brianna brushed the tears from his face. The gesture touched Jake's heart. If only he could express how he felt to Brianna.

Trent remained quiet. Jake said, "I appreciate you both being here. I can't tell you how much."

"Just get better, man. That's all the thanks I need," Trent assured him.

"Same here," Brianna added.

"I'm a little sleepy. Sorry I'm not better company," Jake replied.

"I'll give you two time to be alone. If he needs anything," Trent said, looking in Brianna's direction, "I'll be in the waiting room."

"Thank you for being here," Jake said barely above a whisper.

"Where else would I be?" Brianna asked.

"Oh, I could think of a million other places."

Brianna squeezed Jake's hand and assured him, "I'm right where I want to be."

CHAPTER 24

After Jake dozed off, Brianna left his bedside and went to the waiting room to locate Trent. "There you are. Jake's sleeping now. Give me your number so if anything changes, I can call you," she said.

Trent retrieved a business card and wrote his home and cell phone numbers down. "I can stay."

"He's safe with me. I promise to take care of him."

"You love him, don't you?"

Brianna didn't respond immediately. She wrestled with her emotions. The accident had made her realize she would have hurt if she had lost Jake. "I care about him," she responded.

"Jake's one of the good guys. I think you should give him a chance."

She held out her hand and twisted it. The light from the window hit her ring, causing it to sparkle. "It's complicated."

"I'll mind my own business," Trent said, then left Brianna alone with her thoughts.

Brianna called Bradford. He didn't answer, so

she called Bridget. "I wanted to let you know I am at the hospital with Jake." She explained to her about the accident.

"It's more serious than we thought," Bridget responded.

"No, he's going to be fine."

"I'm not talking about Jake. I'm talking about you," Bridget said. "You've fallen for him."

"I have not."

"Yes, you have. If you didn't care for him, you wouldn't be there."

"What if I do? Aren't I entitled to a little happiness?"

"You've paid a huge cost to be a part of his life. Keep in mind, you're in it for the wrong reasons, and unless you're honest with him and with yourself, your relationship is doomed."

"I thought you didn't like him."

"I don't, but I love you. You're my sister, and although I don't agree with what you're doing, I don't want to see you hurt."

"I know what I'm doing, and I'm not going to get hurt. This is a business arrangement only."

"Keep telling yourself that." Bridget's voice sounded muffled. "That's Matt. I'll talk to you later. Call me if you need me."

Brianna walked past the nurse's station and entered Jake's room. The room's temperature seemed to have dropped. She located an extra blanket in a drawer and used it to cover up with as she sat on the chair next to Jake's bed. She used his control to change the television channel. Before long, she was sleeping. She didn't remain asleep for long, because each time she dozed off, a nurse came in to check Jake's vital signs or to run some tests. She finally got to the point where she could tune them out.

"He cares for you, you know," she heard Joan say as she woke up.

"I guess," Brianna responded as she pulled off the blanket and sat up.

"I know you two didn't get together the conventional way, but give it a chance."

"Can I ask you something?"

"Sure."

"You seem to know a lot about our situation. Do you know why his uncle singled me out?" Brianna asked. If she couldn't get a direct answer from Jake, maybe Joan would give it to her.

Joan seemed to be fidgety. "The reason will be revealed in due time."

Brianna didn't like her response. She hated being the only one in the dark. "Were you and Jake's father close?"

"I was friends with Jack and his wife. I was about ten years younger than them, but we grew up in the same neighborhood."

"Did Jack Banks ever tell you how he knew my father?" Brianna asked.

Joan responded, "Robert Mayfield was your dad, correct?"

Brianna was amazed Joan knew so much. "Yes. Barbara Mayfield was my mom. My name and my siblings' names start with a *B* because of her."

"I didn't know Barbara, but Robert grew up in our neighborhood, too. He was something else."

"I don't know if I want to hear this."

Joan chuckled. "Dear, one thing you youngsters don't realize is that parents are people, too. We had a life outside of what you know."

"It appears that way."

"Anyway, Robert dated my sister in high school. I still remember him, although I was only eight years old. I had a little crush on him," Joan confessed.

"Life really is six degrees of separation."

"It sure is. After he and my sister broke up, I didn't see him too much. I recall a few years later overhearing my sister tell a friend he was getting married. I'm assuming it was to your mother."

"As far as I know, my mom was his first and only wife," Brianna added.

"Jack never mentioned what happened between him and Robert, but whenever conversations came up about people from the old neighborhood and Robert's name was mentioned, he would get quiet."

"I still find it strange I'm mentioned in his will. Besides seeing him briefly while banking at JB Savings and Loan, we had no interaction," Brianna said.

"Jack never did anything without a reason. If Jake knows more than he's letting on, he'll tell you in due time."

Brianna left Joan alone with Jake. She thought about her comments as she washed up in the small bathroom. When she returned, Jake was sitting up. "How's your head this morning?" Brianna asked.

Jake shifted in the bed. "It's better. I can actually sit up without feeling like a hammer is pounding me."

"I was just telling him not to worry about the office. I'll take care of everything. Besides, that's what he pays his VPs for. To handle stuff when he's not there," said Joan.

"I agree with Joan," Brianna said.

Joan stayed for about ten more minutes, then

hugged Jake and bid him farewell. Before exiting the room, she said, "Brianna, before I forget. I've let everyone at the office know that you won't be coming in today, either. Someone has to take care of our Jake." Joan winked her right eye.

"Your first week in your new position and you're already taking off," Jake joked.

"You better be glad you're already in the hospital," Brianna retorted and rolled her eyes.

"Nurse! There's a madwoman in here," Jake said.

"Ooh, you are so wrong," Brianna replied.

She was glad to see Jake in better spirits. After breakfast, the doctor gave him a clean bill of health. "You might experience headaches for the next few days. If they last longer, I need to see you in my office."

"Don't worry. If the pain gets to be too much, I'll be calling," Jake responded.

"Well, young lady, I'm releasing him into your care. Do you think you can handle it?" asked Dr. Razi.

"Call me Nurse Brianna."

A few hours later, Brianna walked through the door of her house. She was only there to pick up some clothes and a few other items. She would be working remotely from Jake's house for the next few days, or at least until he could start doing stuff on his own without fear of fainting.

She slid her suitcase in the back of the car, then jumped in the driver's seat. Jake's eyes were closed. She turned the car on and headed to his house. Traffic wasn't heavy, so it didn't take her long to get there. Jake tried to help her with her bags, but she wouldn't let him.

"You need to worry about getting inside. I got this. Don't make me get my whip out," Brianna said.

"I love a controlling woman."

A man dressed in a black tuxedo-style uniform opened the front door and walked out to assist her. She let him, although she was curious as to who he was. They followed him into the house.

"Who is that?" she asked Jake.

"That's Anthony. He works for me part-time. When he heard about the accident, he insisted on coming over."

"What do you need me for, then? He can take care of you."

"He can't stay twenty-four-seven. He has a wife and kids."

"But still. You should have told me."

He surprised her by reaching for her. "I feared you wouldn't come over if you knew about Anthony."

Brianna pouted. "Your assessment is correct." She picked up her pace and followed Anthony to the guest bedroom. "Thanks, Anthony."

She couldn't be mad at Jake, but still, she felt like she had been tricked. After showering and changing clothes, she found Jake lying in bed. His eyes appeared to be closed. She stood in the doorway and watched him for a few seconds before turning around to walk away.

Jake's headache was the result of his car accident, but Brianna's head hurt because of her conflicting emotions. She found herself falling head over heels in love with Jake and relinquishing the idea of revenge. She said, barely above a whisper, "Daddy, please forgive me."

CHAPTER 25

"I'm not asleep," Jake cried out.

"I wasn't sure and didn't want to disturb you." Brianna turned back around and entered the room.

He patted the bed. "It's big enough for both of us."

"No, buddy. I'm not falling for that trick."

"I couldn't do anything even if I wanted to. This medicine makes me feel groggy, and when we do it for the first time, I want to be one hundred percent."

"Keep on fantasizing, because we won't be doing it."

"We'll have to see about that."

Before Brianna could respond, Anthony walked in, holding a tray of food. "Yours is downstairs. I didn't know if you wanted to eat in your room or at the dining-room table."

"I think I'll eat at the table," Brianna replied.

She left Jake and Anthony alone. "She's a keeper," Anthony commented.

"Yes, she is. Thanks for coming on such short notice."

"That's what you pay me for," Anthony responded.

"Times like these I miss Uncle Jack."

"He was a fine man. You're growing into a fine one yourself."

"You're not just saying that because I'm sitting here in this bed, are you?"

"Now, you should know I don't ever say something I don't mean. Never have and never will."

Anthony soon left Jake alone with his thoughts. He wasn't hungry but knew he needed to eat to keep up his strength. He soon found himself dozing off. When he woke up, he was surprised to find Brianna lying across the bed, typing on her laptop.

"I didn't disturb you, did I?" she asked as she faced him.

"No. This medicine has me sleeping one minute and needing to run to the restroom the next."

He got out of bed to head to the connecting bathroom. When he returned, she was sitting up in the bed. Brianna's actions showed him she cared more about him than she wanted him to know. Once he was back to full strength, they were going to have the conversation Jake had been avoiding. He would reveal his feelings to Brianna, and he hoped she would admit to feeling the same way.

The next few days went by fast. Brianna stayed around to make sure he was okay. His recovery was due to her attentiveness. Once he was able to sit up longer than an hour at a time, he had Joan set up conference calls with his staff. Joan stopped by a few times to check on him, but he assured her that Brianna and Anthony were taking good care of him.

By the end of the week, Jake was back to his old self. He had a dose of cabin fever. Brianna was in his den on a conference call. He got out one of his golf clubs and practiced hitting a ball. He was in mid-swing with the golf club when he heard Brianna clear her throat. "Caught you."

He barely missed hitting the lamp shade. He knew the moment Brianna realized he was fine, she would be leaving. He pretended to be weaker than he actually was, but he had been caught. "I . . . I," he stuttered.

"You're fine, and I'm going home tonight."

He ran behind her. "Please don't go. Stay one more night."

"I miss my bed."

A disturbance downstairs stopped them from continuing their conversation. "I know he's here. I heard about his accident, and I just wanted to stop by," said a female voice.

Jake heard Anthony reassure the unwelcome guest that he would deliver the message.

Brianna looked at Jake. "Looks like you have company. Good thing, too, because I'm leaving." She walked down the stairs.

Jake followed Brianna, and unfortunately, Samantha caught a glimpse of him and pushed past Anthony. "I've been so worried about you. I would have come sooner, but I didn't want to intrude."

"Like you're doing now," Anthony stated.

Jake said, "Anthony, I got this."

e walking in these shoes," she said as the valet
ened their doors.

"I'm looking for Bridget Toliver's table," Bri-
na told one of the hosts at the front door.

"Right this way," said the host.

The music boomed throughout the place. "Girl,
the staff members are men," Tosha observed.

"And fine at that," Brianna responded.

The host opened the door to the main room,
d Brianna jumped as the crowd yelled, "Sur-
ise."

Bridget stood in the center of the room. "We
uldn't let you get married without a party."

Brianna was in shock. She knew Bridget wasn't
ly supportive of her upcoming marriage, so
her to throw a party meant a lot.

Tosha pulled her into the crowd of women.
ome on. You know how we do."

Bridget placed a tiara on Brianna's head. She
gged her. "I know this might not be your last
rriage, but it is your first, and I want you to
e some good memories."

Brianna wiped her eyes. "You're going to make
cry. I can't believe you have me crying."

osha pulled them apart. "Let's party."

rianna mouthed the words *thank you* and was
to the center of the room. She sat in the dec-
ted chair and looked around. Several of her
nds and a few relatives were there.

ridget yelled to get everyone's attention. "We
ld normally play some games, but since this
a normal party, we wanted to get right to the
on."

osha added, "Yes. And first up is Chocolate
nder, Hear Me Roar."

noise sounding like thunder erupted, and Bri-

Anthony frowned. "If you need me, I'll be in
the kitchen."

Jake grabbed Samantha's arm and led her to
the front door. "You need to leave."

"Why? Because your fiancée's here? I saw the
trick's car outside," Samantha answered.

"Don't talk about my baby like that," Jake
snapped.

"I can't believe you! Does she know you were
sleeping with me up until a couple of weeks ago?
Does she?" thundered Samantha.

"I thought you got rid of the trash," Brianna
said.

"Yes, your man's been sleeping with me,"
Samantha yelled.

"That may have been the case, but what's important is he's not sleeping with you now. So, like
he said, I think it's time for you to leave," said
Brianna.

Jake opened the door. "Sam, thanks for checking on me. As you can tell, I'm just fine." He
pushed her out the door as she protested and
closed it.

Brianna laughed. "I have to give it to her. She
doesn't give up."

"She should. I have who I want," he said as he
wrapped his arms around her. He kissed her, lift-
ing her off her feet.

She pulled away. "Jake, we shouldn't do that
again. It's making things c-complicated," she
stuttered.

"Do you want me, Bri?" The fire burned in
Jake's eyes.

"Jake. Let's not—"

Jake didn't wait for her to complete her sen-
tence. He pulled her back toward him, and this

time his tongue invaded her mouth, and Brianna temporarily relinquished control. The kiss ended.

Brianna wiped the lipstick from Jake's mouth with her fingers and answered his original question. "Yes, yes, Jacob Banks, I want you."

CHAPTER 26

Life for Brianna could be descr[...] word—hectic. Between trying to p[...] served her promotion and working [...] ding coordinator for her upcoming [...] barely had time to breathe. She had [...] the phone with Bridget and was on [...] the door when Tosha walked in her [...]

"Where are you headed?" Tosha [...]

"I'm meeting Bridget at Club R[...] feel like going, but she insisted I c[...]

Tosha decided to invite herself [...] me in."

"I'll be ready in a few minutes. [...] my computer off."

A few minutes later, they were [...] garage. "I'll follow you to your p[...] we can drive over together," Tosh[...]

"Sounds like a plan to me."

An hour later, they were pullin[...] ing lot of Club Royale. There [...] cars. Tosha opted to use the va[...]

anna's mouth watered at the sight of the six-foot, buffed man with short dreadlocks making his way toward her chair. "Are you the one getting married?" he asked as he gyrated his body in front of her.

She didn't have to answer, because Tosha said "Yes" for her.

Brianna sat back and enjoyed the show as several other dancers made their way into the room. The crowd was pumped up, throwing dollars everywhere. In between watching the dancers and eating, Brianna enjoyed herself.

She went up to Bridget and hugged her. "Thanks for the party. It's been wild."

"Only the best for you. baby girl." Bridget held up her glass of soda and handed Brianna a glass. They clinked glasses.

"Okay, everyone, it's time to open up the presents," Tosha yelled from across the room.

Two hours later, Tosha and several others were loading Brianna's presents in Tosha's car. "You could have told me what Bridget was planning," Brianna said as they drove to her place.

"And have your sister beat me? I don't think so." They both laughed.

Tosha helped her carry the things into her apartment. Once Tosha left, Brianna took the time to let the night's event soak in.

"I'm getting married," she said as she went through the gifts again. She had plenty of sexy lingerie. "Too bad I won't be using it." She held up a see-through red one-piece. "Then again, I just might."

She closed her eyes and imagined wearing it. She imagined Jake's response. How he would drool and couldn't resist taking it off her. How he would slide it off her shoulders and kiss her neck. How his lips would trail up her thighs. She blinked her eyes a few times, bringing herself back to reality. She folded the lingerie and put it back in the box. She picked up the edible body paint and read the ingredients on the jar. She forced herself not to go back into her fantasy world.

One of her rules was no sex, but she didn't know how long it would be before she broke it. Her original plan seemed to be lost in the wind. Her feelings for Jake had her caught up in her own web of deceit. Her need for Jake's love over-shadowed the need for revenge. She had decisions to make. Maybe she was crazy for going along with Jake to save his company. Who was going to save her from the heartache if things didn't work out when the year was up and they had to go their separate ways?

CHAPTER 27

"Man, I can't believe I let you talk me into coming here," Jake said as he walked into a local strip club with Trent.

"This is your last weekend of freedom, so I thought I would treat you. Don't know when we'll get to hang out again."

A few half-naked women danced near them. Conversation ceased between them as they watched the display. "What were you saying?" Jake asked.

"How I'm glad I'm not giving up my single life." Trent pulled out some money and placed it in some of the ladies' thongs.

Some mutual friends of Jake and Trent showed up, and they partied until the break of dawn. Jake's head felt the full effect of his night of drinking the next morning. He staggered to his medicine cabinet and located some ibuprofen. He took a few and gulped down some water. He did a double take when he saw his reflection in the mirror. His bloodshot eyes stared back at him.

The phone rang. He jumped. The noise seemed

a little too loud. "Coming," he yelled out as he stumbled toward the phone.

"Open up your front door," Brianna said on the other end of the line.

"Bri, today's not a good day."

"I'm outside your door. Now open up," she yelled.

He pulled the phone away from his ear. He found his shades and put them on. She looked radiant on the other side of the door, wearing a tight pair of jeans and a bright yellow shirt and holding a few bags. "What are you doing here?"

"We have a few things to go over before next week."

"I forgot. Sorry. I had a long night."

"I can tell." She fanned in front of her nose. "You might want to go take a bath. And what's with those shades?" She reached up and removed them. The sight of his bloodshot eyes made her say, "Ugh. Put them back on."

"My boys had something of a bachelor party for me."

"Ugh. You definitely need to take a shower. Are the hoochies still here?" She walked past him as if she were looking for someone.

"I'm saving myself for you," he said as he wrapped his arm around her waist.

She pulled away. "Get a bath and a tooth-brush, and I might kiss you."

Jake took her advice. About forty-five minutes later, he came back downstairs. She had food spread out on the dining-room table. "Smells good in here," he said as he took a seat.

"I'm almost through making the salad, and then we can eat."

"So what did you do this weekend?"

"Oh, nothing. Got together with my sister and some friends on Friday night."

"Any male dancers involved?" He was curious. He didn't want his woman—yes, he thought of Brianna as his woman—around half-naked men.

"If you disclose what happened at your little boys' get-together, then I will tell you about mine," she said as she placed salad on two plates.

"That's not fair."

She winked at him. "I can tell you this. I got a lot of sexy lingerie."

He licked his lips. "I can't wait to see you model them for me."

"Keep dreaming, baby. I plan on taking those things back and exchanging them for something else."

"See? That's not fair. Those women spent their hard-earned money trying to find something to please me, and you're going to take it back."

She sat down across from him. "There is this one outfit I think you would absolutely love."

"Describe it to me."

"It's see-through."

"Love it already."

"I haven't finished."

"I can't get past the see-through. You and see-through. Somebody pass me some water, because it's hot in here."

"You're so silly."

"You bring it out in me."

Brianna and Jake took turns passing each other dishes as they piled food on their plates. They barely talked, until Brianna asked, "When can I start moving my stuff in?"

Jake looked up from his plate and answered,

"Anytime. Just let me know when you're ready to have the movers come by to pick up your stuff."

"I need to decide what's coming and what stuff I'll be giving away, so the beginning of next week should be fine."

"I'll get Joan on it."

They ate in silence. Brianna broke the silence by saying, "I would like to redecorate. I will be the lady of the house, and I feel it should reflect my tastes."

"Some things belonged to my parents or my uncle, so before you go getting rid of things, you'll need to consult with me."

"That's fair."

"What? No attitude? No objections?"

She tilted her head before responding, "I'm not all bad."

He laughed. "Baby, I'm just kidding. Calm down."

"I'll be calm once this wedding is over with. We should have just eloped to Vegas or gone to a justice of the peace."

Jake disagreed. "I've always wanted a wedding, so we might as well do it up."

"I've wanted a big wedding too, but this is different." Brianna frowned.

Jake put his fork down and reached across the table and placed his hand on top of Brianna's. He looked her directly in the eyes, without blinking. "I hope by now you know I care about you."

Brianna looked away. "Jake, you don't have to pretend. It's just the two of us."

"This may have started off as a business deal, but it's more than that to me now."

"I wish I could be sure of that."

"You can be. All you have to do is trust me."

Brianna laughed. "Jake, let me tell you a little about my history. Something you didn't find out in your background check."

"You had to bring that up again, didn't you?"

Brianna took a sip from her glass. "My track record with men isn't too good. You know about Charles and how that turned out. Let me go back to the first time I got my fill of men lying. I met this guy in college who I thought I was going to marry."

"You've been engaged before?" Jake seemed to hold his breath as he waited for her answer.

"No, we weren't engaged, but I thought we were in love."

"I can't say I'm sorry it didn't work out."

Brianna rolled her eyes. "Anyway, I caught him in bed with this other girl, and since then, it's been hard for me to trust men."

"So besides this guy and Charles, you haven't dated much?"

"No, that's not it. I've had my share of dates. I'm just cautious about who I let into my heart."

"So do you think you could ever let yourself fall in love with me?"

Brianna didn't answer for a moment. "Maybe. Maybe not."

Jake tried to assure her. "I'm not like those other men."

"That remains to be seen," Brianna responded.

"Bri, you can trust me. I'm not your enemy."

She looked him directly in the eyes for a few seconds before responding. "Most men have hidden agendas, but at least yours is all out on the table, right?"

Jake stared back, without flinching. "I know you care, and I'm patient. Time is all I have."

CHAPTER 28

"It's not too late to change your mind," Bridget said as she helped Brianna put on her veil.

Brianna turned to face her. "I have a confession to make. Please don't be upset with me, but I think I'm in love."

"I knew it. You've fallen in love with him."

Brianna's eyes watered. "I've tried not to, but he's been so sweet to me. We've been spending a lot of time together." She went on and on, trying to justify her feelings.

Bridget placed her arm around her. "Call it off. He'll only break your heart. At least you'll have your dignity."

Brianna pulled herself together. "No. If I'm going to end up with a broken heart, I might as well get some money out of it. Leave me alone for a minute. I'll be all right."

Bridget stood up and looked at Brianna. She adjusted the straps on her violet dress. "You are so pigheaded," she said before leaving the room.

As soon as she knew Bridget was out of the room, Brianna retrieved her cell phone. "You sure you want to do this? You haven't found some loophole, have you?" she blurted.

Jake responded, "We're doing this. In less than an hour, you will be my wife."

"Last chance."

"Brianna, get off this phone. Finish getting ready, and I'll see you at the end of the aisle."

She hung up the phone. A part of her felt disappointed. But what did she expect? Did she really think he would confess his undying love? Tears flowed from her eyes and she couldn't stop crying.

Just then Tosha burst into the room, wearing a knee-length violet dress. "Girl, it's standing room only out there."

Brianna used a tissue to wipe her face. Tosha rushed to her side. "Don't cry. I mean, you guys are rushing it, but I don't blame you." She handed Brianna another tissue. "I wish I had the kind of love you two have. This whole whirlwind romance brings tears to my eyes. I'm jealous."

Tosha's long rant gave Brianna time to pull herself together. "I'm fine. It's just last-minute jitters."

The wedding coordinator entered. "Ms. Mayfield. This will be the last time I call you that," she joked. "Everyone's waiting. Ms. Tosha, we're waiting for you, too."

Tosha hugged Brianna and left the room. Brianna stood up and walked in front of the long mirror. She had lucked out on finding this dress, especially since she'd had less than six weeks to find it. A local designer had made making her dress a priority when she'd learned Brianna was marrying the CEO of Banks Telecom. The ivory, sheath-style satin gown with a fish tail and slight slit in the back had a short train. She admired the hand-sown pearls that adorned the diamond-shaped neckline and the French lace sleeves. She touched the matching veil one last time and waited.

Bradford knocked on the door before entering. He wore a black tuxedo with a violet vest to match her wedding colors. He hugged her and kissed her on the cheek. "You look beautiful."

"Don't start. You'll make me mess up my makeup."

He led her out of the room. He said, as they walked, "He doesn't deserve you."

"Now is not the time."

"I just don't want you to make a big mistake."

"It's too late."

"No, it's not. I can go in there and tell them you changed your mind."

"I'm going through with this."

By now they were near the door. Bridget, her matron of honor, and Tosha, her maid of honor, were walking down the aisle. Brianna looked at Bradford. He looped his arm through hers. The wedding coordinator handed her a beautiful bouquet filled with lilacs and other flowers. A local recording artist sang a song as she and Bradford rounded the corner and entered the room.

She tried her best to focus on the end of the walkway and not to look to her side to see all the people who had come to watch her and Jake tie the knot. She heard a few gasps, acknowledging how beautiful she looked. She hoped she didn't slip and fall, because she could feel the four-inch Cinderella shoes wobbling. Last night, when they rehearsed, the walkway hadn't seemed this long.

Jake stood at the end of the aisle, wearing a

white tuxedo and a lilac vest. The smile on his face put her at ease.

Bradford placed her hand in Jake's and said, "I'm entrusting you to take care of my sister." Bradford then took his seat on the first bench, by Matt and his aunt and uncle.

Brianna's hands shook as she walked with Jake to stand in front of the minister. The minister prayed.

Brianna said a silent prayer. *Lord, please forgive me for taking these vows in vain. I do love Jake, and although he says he cares about me, I want him to love me. I want this marriage to be real. I hope you'll forgive me.*

She had rehearsed her lines all morning, but now, as she stood in front of Jake, the minister, and all these people, she couldn't remember a word. Everyone waited for her to talk. She cleared her throat before speaking. "Jake, our meeting wasn't coincidental. It was destiny. I never thought we would be here at this moment in time, exchanging wedding vows, but we are. I confess my love for you in front of our family and friends."

She was glad the veil hid some of her facial expressions. She continued, "I promise to live up to the agreement as your wife. Jacob Banks, I love you and will spend the rest of our time together showing you how much."

CHAPTER 29

Jake's heart skipped several beats as he stood and listened to Brianna's vows. Did she really mean it when she said she loved him? He wished he could tell if she was acting. It was now his turn to recite his vows.

He turned to face Brianna. "Brianna Marie, although our meeting wasn't conventional, I think I fell for you the moment I saw you. You've enriched my life in so many ways. I can't imagine a life without you. I love everything about you, from the way your eyes twinkle when you're sharing an idea to the cute dimples that form when you smile. You've made my world complete. I promise to love you, honor you, and protect you from this day forward."

The minister said, "Rings please."

They exchanged rings, both nervous as they repeated the wedding vows.

The minister said, "By the power vested in me by the state of Texas, I now pronounce you husband and wife. Jacob Adams Banks, you may now kiss your bride."

Jacob removed Brianna's veil. With his index finger, he wiped the tears from her cheeks before leaning down to kiss her. Time stood still when their lips touched. Only after hearing a few people clear their throats did he stop. Folks cheered around them.

The minister said, "Ladies and gentlemen, I present to you Mr. Jacob Banks and Mrs. Brianna Banks."

The crowd cheered as Jake and Brianna made their way down the aisle. When they got to the foyer, Jake leaned over and whispered in Brianna's ear. "I'm a lucky man."

She responded, "That you are."

"There, there. We have people watching," he teased.

They spent the next thirty minutes taking wedding photos.

"I can't wait to get out of these shoes," Brianna said as she slid them off once they entered the limousine.

He took her right foot and massaged it. "Beautiful from head to toe."

"You can stop pretending. There aren't any cameras or folks around," Brianna said as she leaned back in her seat.

His hand slid up her leg. "I don't say things I don't mean."

She leaned forward, and their lips were almost touching. "So your vows, did you mean those?"

He didn't respond.

She said, "That's what I thought." She moved her leg and attempted to put her foot back on the floor, but he was stronger and held her foot in his lap.

"Like I said, I don't say things I don't mean. Now marinate on that."

He massaged both of her feet as the limousine drove them to the location of the reception. He slid her dress up and massaged her calves. Contrary to her attitude, he could feel her body relax.

The limousine driver spoke over the intercom. "We're pulling up now, Mr. Banks."

Brianna placed both of her feet down. She pulled down the visor to make sure her makeup and hair were intact. Jake enjoyed watching her. She might not know this, but tonight she would be his, and it would be willingly.

People cheered as they exited the limousine. The wedding coordinator rushed them into the lobby so they could line up with the rest of the wedding party and greet their guests. Cameras flashed as they shook hands.

"You were complaining about your feet earlier. Imagine wearing these shoes," moaned Jake.

Brianna laughed. "Don't expect a foot massage."

He pouted. "You're not fair."

"Come on. They're playing our song," Brianna said as she took Jake's hand and led him onto the dance floor for their first dance. Luther's voice rang through the room as she placed her head on his shoulder. Their bodies rocked to the beat. He held her close and didn't want to let her go. They danced for several songs straight, until Bradford tapped him on the shoulder.

"Can I have this dance?" Bradford asked.

"If you weren't her brother, I would tell you no," joked Jake. He released Brianna and left her and her brother twirling on the dance floor.

Trent walked up to Jake and handed him a drink. "If I didn't know any better, I would think you two were really in love."

Jake took the drink and clinked his glass with Trent's. "I surely am. Now I just have to convince her."

Trent commented, "You got your work cut out for you."

Jake agreed. It would be a challenge, but he was up for it. Brianna's laughter could be heard over the noise. "Who is that dancing with my wife?"

"I don't know, but whoever it is got her laughing."

"Here." Jake handed Trent his drink and walked back out on the dance floor. He didn't like the fact that some other man could make her respond like that. She never laughed that hard with him.

He tapped the guy on the shoulder. "I would like to dance with my wife now," he said.

"Sure, man. We were just catching up. Congrats, man. She's a good catch," said a younger version of Denzel Washington.

The music changed into something fast paced. Brianna said, "I'm tired. Let's go sit down."

He had to increase his pace to keep up with her. Once they were seated at their table, he placed his arm around her chair and leaned down close to her ear. "Who was that guy?"

"Nobody important."

Bridget and Matt stood nearby, so Jake decided to drop the issue. Jake asked Bridget, "Would my new sister-in-law like to dance?"

Matt and Bridget exchanged looks. Bridget followed Jake to the dance floor. Jake stopped at a spot on the dance floor where he could have a clear view of his table. He was satisfied that Matt sat and talked to Brianna and that the mystery fellow did not reappear.

"I need to warn you. My sister loves you, and if you ever do anything to hurt her, you'll have to answer to me," Bridget said.

Jake swayed to the beat. "I love your sister and have no plans of hurting her."

CHAPTER 30

Brianna watched Bridget and Jake out on the dance floor. Matt was talking to her, but her mind tuned him out as she replayed the brief encounter with Byron. The sight of him had shocked her.

"May I have this dance?" Byron had asked.

Curious as to why he was there, she had agreed. "I'm surprised to see you here," she'd said.

"Remember my cousin Joyce Sanders? She and Jake are on the Dallas Urban Development Committee. She needed an escort, and when I learned you were the bride, I couldn't pass up the opportunity to see you again."

"As you can tell, I moved on," Brianna had snapped.

"Bri, I won't take up too much more of your time, but I wanted to apologize. I hate that things ended the way they did."

"You taught me a huge lesson."

"That incident taught me a lesson, too. Seeing how much pain I caused you, I never cheated on another woman."

"Too bad it took that to happen for you to change your ways."

"I'm sorry."

Brianna had pulled herself together. She had moved on, but she still felt the pain from his infidelity. It seemed like it had happened yesterday. "Thanks for the dance, but I have other people to see."

When she'd noticed Jake and Trent watching, she'd decided to continue dancing with Byron, who tried to diffuse the situation by telling a joke. She'd laughed louder than she had to.

Brianna snapped back into the present when she heard Matt call out her name a few times. She wasn't supposed to be thinking about her past love. Today was her wedding day. Jake should be at the forefront of her mind. She meant every word she'd said when they'd exchanged wedding vows. Although she had loved Byron at one point, her heart now belonged to Jake, whether he knew it or not.

Brianna hoped Bridget wasn't giving Jake too hard of a time. Matt left to use the bathroom, and Trent slipped into the seat next to Brianna. "Where's your fine friend? She's been avoiding me all evening," he complained.

"I stay out of her business."

"I feel you. So when are you going to tell Jake how you feel?"

It amazed her how on point Trent seemed to be. She shifted in her seat. "You need to mind your business."

"Jake *is* my business."

Brianna turned to face Trent. "Let's get something straight. I'm Jake's wife, and I don't need you or anyone else interfering in our lives."

Trent looked in the direction of Jake and Bridget. They were walking toward the table. "I'll be keeping my eye on you," he said as he left the chair to meet Jake.

"Just when I thought you were cool," Brianna stated under her breath. Her body shivered.

Tosha must have seen Trent leave, because she slipped in his chair as soon as he was gone. "There are so many single rich men here," she said as she opened up her clutch and showed Brianna a few of the business cards she had collected.

"You should find your prince somewhere in there."

"But nothing like your Jake."

Jake and Bridget were now at the table. Jake took a seat on the other side of Brianna. Trent returned and sat next to Tosha. After a few toasts, they were served dinner. About an hour later, the wedding coordinator guided the newlyweds to the table that held the four-tier white cake trimmed with purple frosting.

The crowd cheered as they smashed cake in each other's faces. Jake surprised her by kissing some of the crumbs off.

"You're going overboard," she whispered.

"There's more where that comes from."

"Time to throw the bouquet," the wedding coordinator said as the single women in the room gathered together.

Brianna turned around and closed her eyes. She threw the bouquet and turned around to see who would be the lucky woman. She laughed as Tosha and some other woman ran toward the bouquet, only to lose it to a woman who looked to be in her sixties.

The woman threw it at Tosha. "I don't want this thing. I'm not getting married."

Everyone around them laughed. Brianna walked up to Tosha and said, "I guess you're the lucky person."

Next, they posed for a few pictures.

Then the wedding coordinator gathered the single men together. Brianna sat in a chair, and her heart beat fast as Jake slid her garter off. The men weren't as enthused as the single ladies had been. Trent ended up catching the garter. She heard Trent grunt as he was forced to have his picture taken with the garter and Jake. All the while Byron stared at Brianna. Jake saw the exchange of glances between her and Byron. Brianna hoped Jake wouldn't ask her about Byron later, but knowing him, he probably would.

The night was coming to an end. She found her siblings before leaving with Jake. She hugged them. "Thank you both for your support."

Bradford said, "Jake's not as bad as I thought he was. I just wish you two would have met under different circumstances."

"Don't let your guard down. I still don't trust him," Bridget said.

"I'm a big girl. I can take care of myself," Brianna assured them.

Jake approached and placed his arm around her shoulder. "It's time. We'll see you in about a week."

Brianna turned and said, "Make that two weeks. It'll take us a week to recover."

Jake laughed. "I hope you mean that."

"Don't count on it," Brianna teased.

Once behind the closed doors of the limousine, they forgot about the false pretenses. "You almost made me believe you were willing to forgo one of the rules on your list," Jake said.

Brianna rubbed his arm. "This champagne has me a little light-headed, so you might get lucky tonight."

"I don't want to take advantage of a drunk woman."

"Maybe she wants you to."

"Don't play with me."

Brianna placed her arms around Jake's neck and pulled his lips down onto hers. She showed him with her tongue that she was serious. The moans she heard seeping through his mouth increased the desire she had for him. Before long, they were pulling up to the Four Seasons Hotel, and their lip-locking session ended.

"I rented a suite for tonight. This is the place of our first date," he told her.

"You can be romantic when you want to be," she said. Her heart tugged because Jake acted like he really cared.

Jake opened the limousine door and swooped her up in his arms.

"Whoa," she said.

"It's tradition," he said as he carried Brianna over the threshold.

She got lost in his eyes as he carried her to their suite and placed her on the couch. She looked around her and saw that the room was filled with red roses. A trail of red rose petals led to the bedroom. Several trays of food and a bucket containing a bottle of Moët sat on a table near a chaise.

"Tonight I want you to forget our agreement. Tonight, Brianna, be my wife in every sense of the word," Jake whispered, then kissed her on the neck.

Any resistance she had had before went out the window when she felt his soft lips. She gave in to her feelings. She gave in to the fantasy that she and Jake were like all other newlyweds, happily in love on their wedding night. Tonight she would give in, and she'd think about the consequences later.

CHAPTER 31

Brianna's body quivered as Jake teased her with his tongue. Their eyes locked as he raised himself and entered her, with a gentleness that, under normal circumstances, could be mistaken for love. The room's temperature escalated to boiling as their bodies united. With each stroke, Brianna got lost in the fantasy of being Jake's wife.

Jake's moans were sending her over the edge. Her body betrayed her and gave in to the sensation for the third time. Jake followed suit, and before long, they were each snoring. A hand sliding up her thigh woke her. Instead of pushing his hand away, she welcomed his touch. They made love throughout the night; there would be no doubt that their marriage had been consummated.

Brianna woke up the next morning, dazed. It took her a few seconds to realize she wasn't dreaming. The wedding, the sexual encounter with Jake—they were all real. She moved but felt a tug. Jake's arms, wrapped around her waist, held her down.

"Good morning, Sleeping Beauty," he responded, then moved her hair with his free hand and kissed her on the back of her neck.

Sounding groggy, she responded, "I need to use the bathroom." She was sure that that was not the response he'd been hoping for, but she needed to get away. If Jake kissed her one more time, she would lose it, and she needed to gain her composure. Sleeping with Jake had not been a part of the plan.

She got out of bed and made the mistake of looking back. Jake's eyes followed her. His smile melted the hardness around her heart. She wanted to jump back in bed with him, but her bladder saved her. He blew her a kiss. She smiled and ran to the bathroom.

It didn't take long to release the pressure on her bladder; however, she remained sitting on the toilet so she could think. She thought about the past twenty-four hours and how she would get through the next 364 days without sleeping with Jake again.

Falling in love wasn't part of the plan, and unfortunately, she had fallen. She had fallen so deeply, she considered ditching her plan and actually taking a chance and seeing where the relationship with Jake could go. Maybe they could have a regular marriage. Over the past few weeks, she had seen a different side to Jake. Maybe something good could come out of this, after all. She questioned her original motives. Was it right to make Jake pay for the sins of his uncle?

"I need a shower, and maybe things will become clearer," she said out loud.

She undressed and climbed in the shower. The water and soapsuds cascaded down her body.

Brianna closed her eyes and recalled something her father had said months before his death. *Don't be like me. Learn how to forgive.*

His words now haunted her. Brianna's hatred for Jack Banks had infected her to the core. Brianna moaned, "Daddy, I miss you so much." Tears flowed down her face as she came to the realization that no matter what she did, she wouldn't be able to bring her father back.

Revenge had been the driving force behind most of her decisions when she'd started out on this journey. Letting go of the pain would be hard. Brianna had to deal with the grief and find a way to deal with the present. Not sure how long she had been in the bathroom, Brianna climbed out of the shower, put on a robe, and made a vow to herself to see exactly where their relationship could go.

Jake wasn't in the bedroom when she returned. She was about to yell out his name when she heard him laugh. She followed the sound of his voice. The door to another room in the hotel suite was slightly ajar. His back was toward her, but she could see him holding a phone up to his ear.

"The wedding went off without a hitch . . . The first installment helped . . . Now that the wedding is complete, per the will, I should be able to get the second installment . . . Transfer the funds to the primary business account . . . You'll be able to reach me on my cell."

Brianna continued to listen, and the realization that Jake still saw their marriage only as a business transaction hit her like a ton of bricks. It almost knocked the wind out of her as she stood and listened to him talk to, presumably, his lawyer. Her feet were glued to the spot by the door. She didn't try to retreat when Jake turned to face her. Instead, she stood tall and hid the hurt in her heart as he ended his phone call.

Jake walked toward her. "There you are. I was on my way to get you when my attorney called. Seems like everything is all set."

She crossed her arms. "Good for you."

He reached for her, but she pulled back. He looked confused. She walked back into the bedroom. She found her suitcase and took out some clothes.

"We still have a few hours before our flight leaves, so why don't we have some more fun?" Jake asked as he followed her.

Brianna turned around to face him. "Look. What happened last night . . . this morning can't happen again. You just reminded me of why we did this." She paused before continuing. "This is nothing but a business transaction. Look at what happened between us as a bonus. Now back to reality."

She rushed past him, with her clothes, and went back into the bathroom. As soon as she closed and locked the door, the tears flowed from her eyes. She chastised herself for allowing her emotions to take over. To think she had even considered giving Jake a real chance. The honeymoon was over, and it hadn't even been a solid twenty-four hours. How was she supposed to fake being happy with a man who only considered her a means to saving his business? How could she have fallen in love with such a jerk? She had to pull herself together and quick.

CHAPTER 32

Jake couldn't understand Brianna's change of attitude. He had thought they were actually going to try to make their marriage work. She had willingly given her body to him. He knew he didn't imagine the love he'd felt as they made love over and over throughout the night. Brianna had touched a part of his soul, and he could not go back to the way things were before—before having her in his life.

Brianna barely touched her breakfast and didn't seem excited when, instead of taking a commercial airline, Jake surprised her with their own private jet. He watched her as she walked through the cabin. "If there's anything you want, just ask. I made sure we are fully stocked with some of your favorites."

Brianna looked at him, but not without rolling her eyes. "Thanks," she muttered. Instead of sitting by him, she took a seat in the area opposite him. She picked up a magazine, and he knew she wasn't reading it, because it was upside down.

He chuckled.

"What's so funny?" she asked.

"You." He leaned back in his leather seat and watched her, with amusement.

She threw the magazine at him. He ducked just in time. "You're a jerk! You know that?"

"What did I do?" he asked innocently.

"Just when I thought you were human. How could you talk business during what is supposed to be our honeymoon?"

So she does care, Jake thought. He responded, "It was something that needed to be done. I needed to make sure things were in place for when we returned. I still have a business to run."

"This could have been postponed," Brianna said. "It's a waste of money, anyway. It's not like we have a real marriage."

"Our relationship can be what we want it to be. What we've shared is special, and I could care less about the money right now."

"I can't tell," she snapped.

He changed seats and sat next to her. She squirmed in her seat and turned her face toward the window. The flight attendant walked into their cabin to advise them of departure. A few minutes later, the captain announced over the intercom that they were ready to depart to Puerto Vallarta.

Brianna either ignored him or snapped at him during the entire flight to Puerto Vallarta. This was destined to be a honeymoon he would never forget. He hoped the sight of the beaches would calm her enough so that she would at least enjoy the scenery.

A few hours later, they checked into the Vallarta Palace Resort. Brianna lectured him as soon as they entered their plush suite.

"Don't expect a repeat from last night. This here."—she ran her hands up and down her body—"is off-limits. Since we're here, we might as well enjoy the scenery. Don't expect anything more than a good time—minus the sex, of course." She placed her hand on her hip. "Understood?"

He saluted her. "Whatever you wish."

"Oh, and another thing. We're going to do the activities I want to do."

"I'm here to please."

"First order of business is shopping. I packed light, so I need some clothes."

"After you." Jake held the hotel door open.

Jake felt like Brianna's boy toy as they went from one shop to another. His hands were full. He couldn't hold another bag. The more they shopped, the happier it seemed to make Brianna. They were going to be there only a week, but she bought enough stuff to last for a few weeks.

"I'll let you pick out the luggage," she said as they entered a luggage specialty store.

"Wow, thanks," Jake responded.

She pointed to a table. "Sit those bags there. I'll wait while you look."

"You're so kind," he said, hoping she noticed the sarcasm in his voice.

If she did, she ignored it. He looked at the luggage and determined how many suitcases he would need to accommodate her purchases. He wasn't as annoyed as he pretended to be. He could tell Brianna felt something for him. He knew dragging him from store to store was her way of punishing him.

Brianna's plan backfired, because he enjoyed watching her try on the different outfits and model for him. It turned him on. He regretted she felt adamant about not repeating the previous night's sexual escapade. It would be hard to sleep in the same bed as Brianna and not want to touch her. It would be a long week of cold showers.

The rest of the week flew by as they enjoyed each other's company. It was hard honoring Brianna's wishes, but Jake did. He felt closer to her now than he had before taking the trip. Going back to Dallas would be a taste of reality they both would have to face—a reality he wasn't looking forward to. He didn't want Brianna to be just his invisible wife; he wanted the real thing. He wanted her mind, body, and soul. He wanted her to give birth to his heirs. He wanted her respect. He wanted her love.

II

LET IT GO

CHAPTER 33

The following week, Jake introduced Brianna to his world. Being in Jake's mansion would take some getting used to. She wasn't accustomed to having someone cook and clean for her. She insisted on separate rooms. Her bedroom was almost as big as the master bedroom. It, too, had its own bathroom. There were perks to being Mrs. Banks. Perks she would take advantage of, and hopefully, when this sham of a marriage ended, with her five million dollars, she would be able to keep up the lifestyle she now enjoyed.

Brianna woke up refreshed on this particular Monday morning. Jake had left a note advising her that he had several important meetings that morning and would meet her for lunch. She wasn't scheduled to go back to work until Tuesday, so she had one day left to enjoy her vacation. After dressing in a new ivory pantsuit and putting on the new string of pearls Jake had bought her while on their honeymoon, Brianna jumped in Jake's Jaguar and decided to pay Bridget a surprise visit.

One of Bridget's nosy neighbors ran onto her porch as Brianna pulled into Bridget's driveway. Brianna waved at the neighbor, who jerked her head around so fast, Brianna couldn't help but laugh.

Bridget, looking flushed, opened the door. "Look at you, Mrs. Banks."

Brianna followed Bridget into the house. "I bought this outfit from some boutique in Addison."

"Must be nice to be rich."

"Let's not go there. What's going on with you? You're not looking too good right now, sis." Brianna sat next to Bridget on the sofa.

"It's just morning sickness. Matt's mom says I'm probably having a girl. When she was pregnant with Matt's sister, she went through the same thing."

"If there's anything I can do to help, just let me know."

"I'll be all right. Matt and I have been wanting a baby for a long time, so I'm not going to let a little morning sickness keep me down." Bridget smiled.

"I don't know if I want any kids after seeing what you're going through."

"What? You don't want a little Jake junior running around?" Bridget joked.

Brianna held up her hand. "Don't curse me like that. I'm counting down until this marriage is dissolved."

Bridget eyed her suspiciously. "Brad and I were discussing your situation, and we still don't know how you marrying Jacob Banks is going to be beneficial to our family."

"I'm getting five million dollars. I'm splitting

it with you two. That's the inheritance that Dad would have been able to leave us if his business hadn't folded due to Jack Banks."

"You're playing with fire. I didn't want to admit this, but I watched Jake at the wedding and the reception. He seems like he really does love you."

"Please. The night after we slept together, he was on the phone with his lawyers, talking about business. The only thing Jake loves is his business, and what I am is a business transaction." Brianna's forehead tensed.

"Calm down, girl. But let's backtrack here. So you've slept with him?"

Brianna interrupted her. "I let him have some of this so he would know what he was missing the other three hundred and sixty-four days of this farce we call a marriage."

"I'm worried about you, sis. I think you've gotten yourself into something that's going to be hard to get out of. If you're honest with Jake now, maybe, just maybe, you can make this marriage real."

"Be honest with Jake about what? He knows the deal. We're doing this to save his precious business."

"You know what I'm talking about. You've been determined to get revenge on the Banks ever since Dad died. I admit I, too, held a grudge. Jake's still not one of my most favorite people, but now, with the baby on the way, I think we should be putting our energy into more positive things. What happened with Dad was unfortunate, but—"

"But . . . nothing. I've gotten sidetracked by this thing called love, but I still haven't forgotten what Jack Banks did to our dad." Brianna paused. Her heart rate increased.

"Let it go."

"I've tried. I really have," Brianna said, looking defeated.

Bridget held her stomach and ran out of the room. Brianna felt bad about upsetting her and followed behind her. She watched as her sister leaned over the toilet, disposing of the food left in her stomach. Then she leaned in the doorway and watched as Bridget brushed her teeth. "I'm sorry if I upset you," Brianna said.

Bridget's mouth curved into a half smile. "It doesn't take much these days."

CHAPTER 34

Brianna woke up an hour before Jake the following morning. She eased her bedroom door open, hoping not to disturb him. She could smell the aroma of food coming from the kitchen as she rushed to the front door.

"You're not going to eat?" Betty, the cook, asked.

"No, Betty. Thanks, though. I need to get to the office early."

"But Mr. Banks insisted that I make your favorites."

"Maybe tomorrow morning," Brianna said, hating to disappoint Betty and hoping her growling stomach didn't betray her.

"Mr. Banks isn't going to be happy."

"He'll get over it," she said as she left Betty standing in the doorway.

She hopped in the car, threw her laptop case on the seat beside her, and headed to work. Only a few people were in the office early. Brianna was glad. She wanted to ease back into work. She went through her e-mail and responded accordingly.

She was reviewing a Word document line by line when she felt someone watching her.

Jake stood in the doorway, holding a plastic container. "Since you were in a hurry this morning, I thought I would bring breakfast to you."

"Thanks. But you didn't have to do that," she responded.

Jake closed the door. "Brianna, we need to talk. Not now. Not here. But later on tonight."

Someone knocked on her door. "Come in," Brianna yelled.

Tosha walked through the door. "Welcome back." She looked at Jake. "Oh, I'm sorry. I didn't interrupt anything, did I?"

"No. Have a seat. I need to catch up on a project," Brianna said.

Jake walked around the desk, and before Brianna could react, he kissed her. She forgot all about Tosha being in the room.

"See you tonight, dear," Jake said as he winked at her. "Tosha, have a good day."

"You, too, Mr. Banks," Tosha responded.

Tosha and Brianna watched him walk out of the room. He closed the door without Brianna having to tell him. As soon as the door shut, Tosha burst out with several questions. "Oooh. Seems like you brought the honeymoon into the office! Where did y'all go? Can I see the pictures?"

Brianna held up her hand. "I don't have time to play fifty questions with you. We got work to do."

Tosha leaned back in her chair and crossed her legs. "My, my, my. For someone who has married one of the finest men in Dallas, you seem a little . . . What's the word? Testy."

"I'd appreciate it if you refrained from talking about my personal life until after hours."

"Let me call Jake and ask him to come back so he can give you some, because your attitude is funky."

"Whatever."

"Look. Call me when you calm down. I'm out." Tosha stood and headed out of the room.

"Wait. I'm sorry. Let's start over," Brianna said.

Tosha sat back down. "I'm listening."

Brianna got animated as she recounted their trip to Puerto Vallarta. She removed a large gift bag from under her desk and handed it to Tosha. "When I saw this, I thought about you."

Tosha acted like a kid at Christmas as she discarded the tissue paper to get to her gift. "Girl, this is beautiful and my birthstone, too." Tosha removed the amethyst necklace and bracelet from the black velvet boxes.

Brianna knew her attitude from earlier had been forgiven when Tosha ran around her desk and hugged her. "Girl, you're the best friend a woman could ever have." She held up her gifts. "There's perks to being Banks's wife's best friend."

Brianna started singing one of Kanye West's hit rap songs. "I ain't saying she's a gold . . ."

"Now all you have to do is introduce me to one of his rich friends."

"You know Trent."

"Girl, I thought *I* was high maintenance. Trent, now, he's a piece of work. I'm sure Jake has other friends."

"Trent's the only one that I know. You got all those business cards. Use them."

"Please, Bri. Jake could give me the inside scoop," Tosha begged.

"No. I'm not getting involved."

"Spoilsport."

"Gold digger."

Tosha relented. "Speaking of gold digging, let me warn you. Folks have been really talking."

"That's what I was afraid of."

Tosha checked the door and turned back to face Brianna. "I hate to be the bearer of gossip, but you need to know what some of these folks are saying behind your back."

"You know what? Folks are going to talk, so let them."

"Just watch your back. The main ones who smile in your face are the main ones talking about you behind your back." Tosha picked up the gift bag from Brianna's desk and left.

Tosha was no longer in earshot when Brianna said, "Tosha, I hope that doesn't include you."

CHAPTER 35

Jake found it hard to concentrate. Overton, his attorney, had just confirmed that the second installment of funds from his uncle's estate was in place and legally he could now move forward with Banks Telecom's research and development. The financial burden had been lifted; however, his heart ached because he wanted Brianna's love.

"Did you get a chance to read the papers I sent over?" Overton asked.

"Not yet," Jake responded while opening up the brown envelope. His eyes had to be playing tricks on him. "How could this be?"

"Jake, you're old enough to know about the birds and the bees. I mean, you did just get married," Overton joked, trying to lighten up the situation.

"Man, I'm sorry. I'm talking out loud. Tara told me the kid wasn't mine. Now I'm finding out years later that he is."

"Your uncle had everything verified before he died. My associate was working on it but had an accident. The file got misplaced, and he just returned to the office, so it's our fault you're just now discovering this," Overton attempted to explain.

"Regardless, it doesn't change the fact that I have a son. Christopher Matthews Spain." He read further down on the document. "Wait a minute. He was adopted. Don't you need both parents' permission for an adoption to go through?"

"There was no father listed on his birth certificate. From what we gathered, it appears Tara had previously tried to claim the adopted father, Byron Matthews, as the birth father. A DNA test taken before she died proved he wasn't."

"I don't know what to say. This here hits me harder than losing Uncle Jack. Me. A father."

"Let it digest a little, and then we can discuss it further."

"Let me ask you this, and then I'll let you go. If I wanted to see him, could you set it up?"

"I'll do my best. You might get some opposition from his adopted parents, but because of the unique circumstances, we might be able to work something out."

"Check on it for me. In the meantime, I got a lot of thinking to do."

They shook hands and Overton left Jake's office.

I have a son. If Tara wasn't already dead, I would kill her. I can't believe she tried to pass him off as someone else's. I asked her if the baby was mine. We took tests, and she showed me the results. If I had insisted the results be sent directly to me, I wouldn't be facing this situation now.

Joan interrupted his thoughts when she entered

his office. "The three o'clock meeting is about to start, Jake."

He glanced at his watch. "I'll be there in a few minutes." He temporarily pushed thoughts of Christopher to the back of his mind. He picked up his briefcase and headed to the conference room on the next floor.

The room got quiet when he entered. Brianna sat at the end of the table, as if she ruled the world. Her whole persona oozed sex appeal. He wiped the sweat from his forehead as he placed his briefcase on the table, took out some forms, and passed them around.

"I want to thank you all for being here. We have a lot to discuss. I have some good news," he said, trying his best to ignore Brianna.

As he disclosed his plans for research and development, he saw the excitement of his staff increase. Seeing Brianna's smile and her dimples made him feel better. He hoped she would carry the positive attitude home with her. The meeting lasted for two hours. Brianna lagged behind everyone else when it was over.

"Congratulations. Things are working out," she said, slipping out before he could respond.

He walked behind her, until he felt Joan's hand on his arm. "Let her go. She'll come around in due time."

"Joan, it's sort of complicated."

"Love can be that way," Joan replied, then left him alone in the hallway.

It was after seven when Jake arrived home. Betty fussed at him about being late for dinner. Brianna sat at the end of the dinner table, eating.

She failed to acknowledge him when he entered the dining room. Jake pretended as if it didn't hurt his feelings, but it did.

"So how was your day?" he asked, hoping to break the ice.

"It was okay. Felt kind of funny, but things will be back to normal in a couple of days."

Jake took his seat and said grace before eating. "You didn't have trouble with anyone, did you?"

"A few snares and stares don't scare me," she responded as she took a sip from her glass.

"If anyone gives you a hard time, let me know and I'll handle it."

"I can handle my own problems."

"I didn't say you couldn't. I just don't want anyone giving you a hard time because of our relationship."

"Don't worry yourself."

Jake stopped eating. He put his fork down. "Bri, as long as you're my wife, your worries are my worries."

"I'm counting the days on the calendar," she snapped.

"Sweetheart, you don't have to be like that. We can make this work."

"Here I thought you were a realist. Wake up from the fantasy, because you and I . . . It's not happening," Brianna responded.

Betty walked in, carrying dessert. "Brianna, I was told peach cobbler was your favorite."

"It is. You're spoiling me." Brianna ignored Jake as she eyed the dessert.

Betty set the cobbler on the table; then left the room.

Jake watched Brianna in amusement. She couldn't fool him. Her attempt to ignore him said more than her words could. He felt rejuvenated. He now felt like he had a chance. He had saved his business; now he set out to save his marriage.

"Bri, remember earlier I said I wanted to talk to you?"

"Can it wait? I ate so much. All I feel like doing now is lying down."

"Go upstairs. I'll stop by your room when I'm through."

He watched her leave the room. His cell phone vibrated, breaking the trance.

"The honeymoon must still be going on, because you hardly have time for your boy these days," Trent said on the other end of the line.

"I've been married for only about three weeks, so stop tripping," Jake responded.

"So tell me. Did you consummate the union, or do you have blue balls?"

"Trent, you need to mind your own business."

"You must not have, because you're too tense." Trent laughed on the other end.

"I'm tense because of Tara."

"Tara? I'm trying to remember her."

"Tara Spain. The one you said looked like Miss America but had an attitude that rivaled a bull."

"Oh yeah. What's up with her?"

"Man, she got killed in a car accident a few years ago."

"Sorry to hear that. I wouldn't wish that on anybody."

"Well, she had a baby and failed to tell me the child was mine."

"Get out of here. You're a daddy? Did you do a blood test?"

"I did all of that three years ago, but I come to find out, Tara altered the results."

"I knew she was a skank."

"Now I got to figure out what I'm going to do. He's my son, so I got to figure out how I can make him a part of my life."

Trent sighed into the phone. "What did Brianna say?"

"I haven't told her yet."

"Good luck with that."

"Speaking of my wife"—Jake stressed the word *wife*—"she is waiting for me upstairs."

"Well, my booty call is waiting for me, so you go get yours, because I'm definitely going to get mine."

After hanging up, Jake headed upstairs and stood in Brianna's doorway. Her eyes were closed, and she was bopping her head up and down. She had changed into a pair of pink, hip-hugging shorts and a small T-shirt. Her breasts appeared to be bursting at the seams. Jake adjusted his pants before walking through the door.

Brianna, I know you didn't sign on for this, but we're about to become parents. I pray Christopher's adopted parents understand, but he's my son, and a son needs his father.

CHAPTER 36

Brianna felt Jake's presence long before he entered the room. His cologne attacked her senses the moment he entered. She kept her eyes shut until she felt Jake's hand brush against her arm. She opened her eyes and removed the headphones from her ears. "So what did you want to talk about?"

Jake sat down on the edge of her bed. "You. Me. Us."

"Do you want to make an amendment to our contract?"

He shook his head no.

Brianna responded, "Then there's nothing for us to talk about."

"We have eleven more months together, so can we—I plead, I beg—can we try to get along? The tension between us is getting to me."

"Really. Well, you haven't seen nothing yet."

She placed her headphones back on her ears. She didn't have the volume up, so it irritated her when he yelled out her name a few times.

She snatched the headphones off of her ears. "What? I'm trying to relax."

Jake repeated to her what he had told Trent earlier about Christopher.

Brianna stared at him in disbelief. "Why did it take three years for you to discover this?"

"I don't have an answer to that."

"I don't know if I can deal with all this." Brianna's hands flew up in the air.

"You're my wife. We're supposed to be in this together."

Brianna was afraid to give in to her feelings. She loved Jake but didn't trust him enough to share all of herself with him. News of a child had her head hurting. "I'm your wife in public, but behind closed doors, this is what it is. Now I'd appreciate it if you would leave my room." She frowned. "And please close the door."

Jake didn't say another word. He left and did as she had asked. When the door shut, instead of feeling relieved, Brianna became frustrated with the uncertainty of their relationship. Having a child thrown into the equation only complicated matters further. She attempted to go to sleep but instead tossed and turned in bed. She expected Jake to return, but he never did.

Brianna decided to go check on Jake. Jake's bedroom door was closed. Light shined from the bottom of it. *I'll talk to him later,* she thought and returned to her room. She closed her door, pulled out her journal, and wrote down the events of the past day. She had several questions about Christopher for Jake. She asked herself, *Am I ready to be a mom? Would the child's adopted parents even let them be a part of his life?* With heavy eyelids, Brianna closed the journal and placed it on the nightstand.

The alarm clock buzzed for a long time before Brianna woke up. She jumped up, hoping to catch Jake. Overnight she had realized she might have been too hard on him. Finding out he was a dad out of the blue had to be stressful. She owed him an apology for the attitude she had given him the previous night. After getting dressed, she went downstairs, and Betty informed her Jake had left a few hours before.

"How can that be? It's only seven," said Brianna.

"He said he had a meeting to prepare for. I try my best not to interfere in his business."

"Did he leave a message for me?" Brianna asked.

"None that I'm aware of," Betty responded as she piled food on Brianna's plate.

Brianna tried not to let her disappointment show. She ate her food and left for work. She could feel depression setting in. While she was still on the road, she called Bradford, hoping he could cheer her up. "Hi, li'l bro."

"Don't talk to me," Bradford teased.

"Brad, I'm sorry. I'm trying to adjust to the married life."

"Forget your family. Forget your friends. That's what you rich snobs do."

Bradford talked to her during her entire trip to the office. By the time she pulled into the parking garage, he had her side hurting from laughing so hard. She could always depend on her brother to cheer her up. She climbed out of her car and hurried inside.

Mark, the security guard, held the elevator for her. "How's it going, Mrs. Banks?" he asked.

"Now, when did we get so formal?" she teased.

"I know how some folks are. I didn't want to be disrespectful."

"Mark, come on. It's me. The same Brianna you've always known."

"Just checking. Have a good day."

"You too," she responded as the elevator doors closed.

She decided to make a detour to Jake's office before heading to hers. Joan was her usual cheerful self. "He's in his office. Go right on in," she said after greeting Brianna.

Jake was on the phone, so she took a seat in the chair across from him and waited until he ended his call. He hung up, and the sparkle that was usually in his eyes wasn't there. "What do you need, Brianna?" he asked.

"I stopped by to see you before getting my day started," she responded.

He looked at the clock on the wall. "You must be running late, because it's after nine. I thought your day usually started around eight."

"It normally does, but I overslept this morning, and you were gone."

"Maybe you need a better alarm clock. I'll make sure I get the old one replaced."

"It wasn't the clock. It worked fine. I didn't sleep well last night," she confessed.

"I can get the mattress replaced if it's causing you not to get any sleep."

"I think I ate too much."

"Can't have that, can we? You do have to watch your figure."

"You think I've put on weight?" Brianna asked.

"Most men love meat on a woman's bones."

"What about you, Jake? What do you like?"

"My opinion doesn't matter."

Brianna changed the subject. "Did you want to talk about your child?"

"When I wanted to talk, you pushed me away. Now I don't feel like talking."

Jake was now giving her the same type of attitude she had given him the night before. Brianna didn't like it. She took a few deep breaths. "About last night, I wanted to apologize."

"Apology accepted. Now, was there anything else?" Jake looked at the clock again.

"No, nothing else," she responded before storming out of his office.

Brianna spent the morning in staff meetings. Being a manager involved more meetings and more paperwork than she'd realized. To say her day wasn't turning out well was an understatement. Her peers were letting their true colors show. Lucky for them, she was a professional; otherwise, she would have said some things to them. She refused to let them or anyone else disrespect her. Contrary to what they thought, she had earned her promotion the right way. With her MBA, she should have been in her current position when she was hired by the company, but that wasn't their business. She had had an ulterior motive for wanting to work there and had had no problems starting off as a project manager.

Now that she was Mrs. Banks, did they really expect her to deal with their blatant attitudes? She only had to say the word, and they would be fired. In fact, she would keep a special folder documenting her peers' actions.

Jake wasn't accepting any of her calls, and that was unlike him. Brianna needed to learn as much as she could about Jake's child and the child's mother. She refused to let the child come in between them.

CHAPTER 37

Jake didn't come home until after nine that night. Brianna purposely left her door open so she could see him come in. She heard him as he walked up the stairs. He didn't bother to stop by her room to speak to her. Her light was on, so she had no doubt he could have at least stuck his head in the door to check on her.

His door slammed shut, and it irritated her. Brianna threw her journal on the nightstand before setting her alarm clock to wake her up an hour earlier than her normal time. She tossed and turned the entire night. By the time she got downstairs the next morning, Jake was gone. His bad attitude had gone on long enough. She was determined to get to the bottom of things.

Brianna decided to work from home so she could do some snooping around. She sent out a broadcast message to her staff, informing them that she would be available by cell phone if they needed her. Maybe Jake was hiding something else. It was about time she got better acquainted with her surroundings.

Since it was the middle of the week, the house staff was off, so she could snoop at her leisure. She acquainted herself with each room. She saved Jake's office for last. The first thing she did in there was look for a secret compartment. Most people of Jake's status had them. She removed book after book on the bookshelf but was unable to find anything.

She sat at his desk and twirled around in the big burgundy leather chair. His office line rang. She wondered who would be calling in the middle of the day, when most folks knew he would be in the office and, at the very least, would have tried him on his cell phone. Curiosity got the best of her, and she answered the phone.

"Banks residence. How may I help you?"

"Is Jake there?" a female voice asked on the other end.

"I'm sorry, but Mr. Banks is not available. Would you like to leave a message?"

"This is Kandie Reins. Please let him know I'm back in town."

"I'll give him the message."

"Who am I speaking with, if you don't mind me asking?" Kandie asked.

"No, I don't. This is Mrs. Banks."

"Mrs. Banks? I thought Jake told me his mother was dead."

"She is. This is Mrs. Banks, his wife," Brianna responded.

Silence.

"Hello," Brianna said a few times.

The phone clicked. Less than ten minutes later, the phone rang again. She picked up.

"Why are you answering my business line, and

why aren't you in the office?" Jake asked, sounding upset on the other end.

She stuttered, "I . . . I, well . . . You're the one trying to hide something."

"I don't have time for games. I have a business to run."

"I'm working from home, because I feel like it. I'm in your office because you have a big desk and an Internet connection. Now how was I supposed to know one of your hoochies was going to call?"

"We'll talk when I get home."

"I'll probably be asleep when you get home."

"Tonight I'll make it a point to come home early."

"Please don't come home early on my account."

"I got some people waiting for me. I'll see you later." Jake hung up.

Brianna wondered why he had an attitude with her. He was probably upset because she had messed things up with Kandie. Jake was her man now, and she had no plans of giving him up. Then again, if, after a year, he wanted out, she wouldn't stand in his way. She didn't want a man who didn't want her.

An idea crossed her mind. She turned to the address and phone number section of her organizer. She needed someone to help her with her dilemma. She was not going to sit here and let Jake hurt her. She had to do something to protect her heart. If the marriage was going to end, it would end on her terms, not his. She pulled out her cell phone and left a message for an old college buddy.

Brianna's investigation didn't result in any new information, so she spent a few hours working on reports. Tired and hungry, she decided she would venture to the kitchen. She went to the gray steel refrigerator to see if she needed to make a trip to the supermarket. The kitchen looked like it could have been right off the pages of *Better Homes and Gardens,* with its marble countertops and steel stove and range. The fully stocked refrigerator offered many choices. Brianna chose to cook something quick and easy—steak and potatoes.

"Something smells good," Jake said as he entered the kitchen.

Brianna stirred sugar into the pitcher of lemonade. "I hope you don't mind."

"This is your kitchen as long as you're here."

"I thought we would eat in here for a change. The dining room can be so formal."

"Let me wash up, and I'll be back."

She set the table in the kitchen and placed the food on the plates and poured their drinks. The table was set and ready by the time Jake returned. They ate while talking about things at the office. Brianna felt relieved they were talking. She didn't forget about Kandie's phone call earlier.

"So who is Kandie?" she asked.

"Kandie is someone from my past. You don't have to worry about her calling again."

"So how did she take it when you told her you were no longer available?"

"Believe it or not, she congratulated me. We used to kick it, but her business requires her to travel a lot, so we hardly saw each other."

"Kandie, Samantha. What other women should I be concerned about?"

"Bri, you're a handful. I have no time for any other women. Believe that."

Brianna held up her butter knife. "Don't make me cut you."

"I like a ride-and-die chick."

"Man, you're crazy." Brianna laughed.

"I got the dishes. Why don't you just sit and talk to me?" Jake said.

"I'll wait for you to finish. You might want to throw a plate at me or something," she joked. Brianna hummed the lyrics to one of Rihanna's songs. "I'm breaking dishes up in here . . ."

Jake washed, while she dried. "You know, it's strange learning you have a son," he said.

"So were you and his mom close?" Brianna asked.

"We had our fling."

"I'm surprised a playboy like yourself took chances like that and didn't use a condom."

"Oh, I didn't play Russian roulette. The condom burst. I use a condom with every woman I'm with."

"You didn't use one with me."

"You're my wife."

"But still. We didn't have the talk about sexually transmitted diseases. We both could be in danger."

"I have a clean bill of health. Do you have any diseases I should be concerned about?"

"No. That's not the point. It's the fact that we both were so careless. Next time we're using a condom."

Jake splashed dishwater on her by accident. "So you're admitting there's going to be a next time?"

Brianna wiped the water off her arm. "I didn't mean to say all that. Just speaking hypothetically."

"You won't get any complaints from me if we do. Like Marvin, I need some sexual healing."

CHAPTER 38

Brianna put her hands on her hips. "Back to Kandie and Samantha. Let's get this clear. No women. Period. If you get horny, you better jack off, because if I find out you've been messing with someone, our little deal is off." She sat down at the table.

"Calm down. I have no reason to look outside of our relationship. Contrary to what you might think, I am a man of my word."

"I'm just saying, I'm not going to let you disrespect me."

Jake dried off the last dish and went and sat at the table, across from Brianna. "Bri, you're the only woman I want."

Brianna confused him. One moment she was hot; the next cold. She was like a Dr. Jekyll and Mrs. Hyde. His emotions were invested in their relationship, and he wanted nothing more than to swoop her up into his arms. He loved Brianna, and there was no getting around it anymore. Many women had loved him, and he'd left them; now he felt the pain they'd surely felt.

* * *

The look on Brianna's face wasn't one of anger but desire. Jake tried his best to resist reaching over and kissing her. He wanted her. His body needed her to quench the thirst only she could satisfy.

"I need to go take a shower," he blurted and rushed from the room. He stayed in the shower longer than he'd anticipated. When he got out and walked into his bedroom, he blinked his eyes several times as he stared at the mirage of Brianna's naked body draped across his bed. He questioned his state of mind.

"What are you waiting for?" Brianna asked.

He didn't want the dream to end, so he obliged the mirage. Jake knew he wasn't dreaming the minute his lips touched Brianna's and she didn't disappear like a mirage. Without waiting for him to make the next move, Brianna removed a condom from a package. He put it on while she watched.

Brianna pulled him on top of her. Their bodies united as one once again, reminding Jake of how he had felt on their wedding night. The feelings he had been holding back were released. He told Brianna over and over how much he loved her. He didn't care anymore. He wanted her to know how he felt. She could run away from her feelings, but he had decided to face his head-on—no matter what the consequences.

They made love several times throughout the night. When Jake woke up the next morning, the spot where Brianna had lain was empty. He called out to her but didn't get a response. Her fragrance lingered in the air. It took him some time to get enough energy to leave the bed. He showered and dressed in record time, then went to find her. He smiled when he heard her singing in her bedroom. He knocked on the door.

"Good morning," Brianna said. The sight of her standing in nothing but her underwear sent a jolt through his body.

"Why don't we ride into the office together?"

"I would, but I'm meeting up with an old college buddy of mine later, so it's probably best that I drive my own car," Brianna responded.

Jake didn't want to argue. The memories from last night were enough to have them both in a good mood, and he didn't want to spoil it. He relented and left her to get dressed.

"I'm surprised she let you out to play," Trent said to Jake while they were playing a video game over at Trent's place.

"You know we don't have a typical marriage," Jake responded.

"I can't tell. We haven't hung out since you said 'I do.'"

"I'm a busy man. I'm just trying to keep it all together."

"The best of both worlds. A fine woman at home and a thriving business."

"Business is looking up, but I don't know about the woman."

"Jake, come on now. A man doesn't have the kind of smile on his face like the one you have on yours unless he's getting satisfied at home."

"I need to talk to someone, and you know more than anyone. It's hard. One minute she acts like she cares about me, and the next minute she's giving me the cold shoulder. It's wearing me out."

"Keep wearing her out in the bedroom. I bet you she comes around."

"Brianna is different from any other woman I have met. She doesn't cater to me because I'm Jacob Banks. In fact, she seems to make me work harder because I'm Jacob Banks."

"You got it bad. Never thought I'd see you go out like this, man. Here's to a happy marriage and another whooping, because, Jake . . . this game is over," Trent said as he made a touchdown, winning the game.

Jake threw the control down. "I hate when you win."

"I won't rub it in your face this time. You got a lot on your mind. What are you going to do about your son?" Trent offered him another drink.

Jake took it and said, "I spoke with the attorney. He tried to set up a meeting with the adopted parents, but they refused, so we're taking it to court."

"When do you go to court?"

"Overton says it may be a few months, so until then I'll make sure I do everything I'm supposed to do so I can bring my son home."

"How does Brianna feel about all of this?"

"We talked about it, but she didn't say much."

"What if she doesn't want him around?"

"That's a bridge I'll cross if I come to it. First, I have to make sure I get my son. I grew up without a dad, but my son won't."

III

WHAT'S LOVE GOT
TO DO WITH IT?

CHAPTER 39

"Bri, I can't believe you're asking me to do this. Are you sure?" asked Lisa Green, Brianna's old college friend. Lisa hadn't changed much since college, except her hair, once shoulder length, was now cropped, accenting her long eyelashes. She stood five feet two inches and that was with heels and she seemed to be in top shape.

"I'll have the cashier's check waiting for you the moment it's a done deal."

Lisa drank her margarita. "I have to be honest with you. If Jacob Banks was my husband, there is no way I would be handing him over to another woman on a silver platter."

"It's only a test. I want to see how far he'll go. I want to see how committed he is to me."

"Promise me you won't get mad if he wants to go all the way."

"Lisa, we've been friends for too long for me to let a man come between us."

"Let me know when and where to show up, and I'll make the rest happen."

"Thank you, Lisa. You're the only one I can trust to do this for me."

Brianna hugged Lisa, and then they went their separate ways. She hoped Jake would be able to pass the test. She checked her messages. Jake had filled her voice mail with several messages. After listening to them, she thought, *You're making this hard. But I have to do what I have to do. If we're going to make this marriage work, our relationship has to be solid. I have to know I can trust you.*

Brianna stopped giving Jacob attitude. She wanted his guard to be down as she executed the next phase of her plan. He had confessed his love for her during their last lovemaking session; however, Brianna knew never to believe what a man said during the heat of ecstasy. She waited and waited for Jake to make the confession again, but as their two-month anniversary approached, he never did.

The love she felt for Jake had grown. The pain she felt tugging at her heart over the situation with his child had also grown. She wondered how much longer she could go on pretending not to care. She had given Lisa Jake's schedule, and now she only had to wait for her to make her move. Lisa moved fast.

Lately, Jake had been coming in later and later. She missed their late-night conversations, which always ended with her sending Jake to his room. Every time she asked him about his son, Christopher, Jake's responses were vague.

On this particular night, Brianna made it a point to stay up late. She waited downstairs. She pretended to be engrossed in a movie when Jake walked through the door.

"Hi, Bri. I thought you would be asleep by now."

She uncrossed her legs. "I couldn't sleep, so I decided to come downstairs to watch a movie."

"Is something wrong with the TV in your room? If so, I'll get it replaced."

"No. I just wanted a change of scenery." She looked between him and the movie.

"I had another late-night meeting."

"You've been having a lot of those lately," she commented, hoping he couldn't detect any hint of jealousy.

"This new client—well, she's not a client yet—keeps putting us through hoops, but I'm about to tell her to take her business elsewhere."

"Don't do that. Remember what you told me. You never turn down business."

"That was before I met Lisa Green. The woman is ruthless." By now Jake was sitting next to her on the sofa.

"You're a big man. I'm sure you can handle her."

"Can I get a back rub?" he asked.

Brianna stretched her arms out wide and yawned. "I'm sleepy. You'll have to get a rain check on that back rub."

She left him sitting on the sofa, wondering why she had abruptly left. She rushed upstairs. She closed her door and dialed Lisa's number. "You're doing good. Just keep at him, and he'll be putty in your hands."

"Bri, I don't feel good about this," complained Lisa.

Brianna ignored her reservations. "Don't worry about it. Just so you know, I haven't been performing my wifely duties, so your next meeting should be at your house. On second thought, I'll rent a condo and e-mail you the address. Have him come over, and make your move."

"You still have time to change your mind. He's been resistant to my passes so far, and if we aren't discussing business, he talks about you."

Brianna felt relieved, but she had come this far to test Jake, so she might as well see it through. "The plan is still a go. Look for an e-mail later this week with the details."

Brianna heard a knock on her door. She hoped Jake hadn't overheard her conversation. She slid under the covers, just in case he happened to peek in her room before going to bed. Sleep didn't come easy for her. The thought of Lisa seducing Jake haunted her.

"Bri, wake up. You're dreaming," Jake said as he held her in his arms. "I heard you sobbing all the way in the hallway. What were you dreaming?"

It took Brianna a few seconds to pull herself together. She wouldn't dare describe her nightmare to Jake. "I don't remember," she lied.

Brianna wanted to feel Jake's arms around her every morning, but she wouldn't allow herself the joy. Their relationship had resulted from a business deal, nothing more, nothing less. As much as she wanted to trust Jake fully, Byron's betrayal seemed to creep up in her mind. Brianna had to do whatever she could to protect her heart. Pushing Jake into the arms of another woman would be a test of his fidelity and possibly the cure to her aching heart.

CHAPTER 40

Jake loved Brianna, but her refusing to sleep with him was making it hard on him physically. He had never gone over a month without sex, and now that he was a married man, he felt like he shouldn't have to go a week without it if he didn't want to. Brianna's actions confused him. One minute she acted as if she loved him, but the next, she acted as if she wanted to bury him six feet under. If Dr. Phil were to diagnose their relationship, he would consider it unhealthy to the highest degree.

Overton placed some papers in front of him. "If you'll sign here, that's all I need. It's been a few months, but finally, we're close to getting your case in front of a judge."

Jake signed the bottom of the first page. He picked up the picture of Christopher that Overton had given him. Christopher mirrored him at the same age. "I can't wait to meet him."

"It's not fair for them to keep you from your child, but the judge I'm trying to get is said to be fair."

"I hope this doesn't get ugly."

"What will help is if you and Brianna show a united front."

"I'll have a talk with her, because I want my son."

Joan said over the intercom, "Your five o'clock appointment is here."

Overton stood up. "I'm about to leave, so if you need anything else, let me know." He paused. "Oh, one more thing. Do you two plan on staying married after the one year?"

"I do. It all depends on Brianna."

"Let's hope this custody battle is over with before the year is up. Because we don't need any surprises."

Jake stood up and shook his hand. "I appreciate all you're doing."

Joan met Overton at the door. "Jake, I'm about to head out," she said.

"Send Ms. Green in," said Jake.

Lisa walked in, looking like she had stepped off the cover of a fashion magazine. Jake cleared his throat a few times as she sashayed by and took a seat across from his desk. "Sorry, I'm late, but the traffic in this town is so unpredictable," she said as she crossed her legs, revealing her beautiful brown thighs.

Brianna's face flashed in his head several times; however, Lisa's voice reigned in his ears.

"It's late. Why don't we take this meeting to my place? I'm hungry. Aren't you?" Lisa asked.

"I can always order something and have the security guard bring it up."

Lisa moved closer to the desk, revealing her cleavage. "I'm this close"—she used her hands to measure—"from closing the deal. Just one dinner. I have some rental property not far from here." She wrote down her address. "I'll meet you there."

Lisa didn't wait for him to respond. She grabbed her purse and pranced out of the room. As soon as she was out the door, Jake released his breath.

. He dialed Brianna's cell phone number. "What's for dinner?"

"I've already eaten. I can whip you up something if you like."

"Where's Betty?" he asked.

"I gave her the night off. I wanted some alone time."

"Well, that's okay. I'll get something while I'm out."

"What time should I expect you home?" Brianna asked.

The thought of lusting for Lisa made him feel guilty.

"Jake, are you there?" Brianna asked.

"I'm not sure. I'm meeting up with a client, and it depends."

"You just asked me about dinner." She paused. "Never mind. See you when I see you." She disconnected the call.

Do I sense some frustration on her part? He asked himself. He shook his head several times. No, he was not falling for it. He hoped he didn't slip up and do something stupid. If he did and Brianna found out, he would not only lose her, but he would forfeit the rest of his inheritance. He would rather lose the money than lose Brianna at this point, though. He picked up the piece of paper with Lisa's address and headed out the door.

It didn't take Jake long to get to Lisa's condo.

She led him into her spacious yet beautifully decorated living room. "This is nice," he commented.

"Glad you like it," Lisa said as she led him into the dining room. Two candles were lit, and several entrées and side items adorned the table.

"I didn't know what you wanted, so I decided to give you choices," she purred.

He wondered how she had had time to cook this. He was sure she had had this little scenario planned long before coming to his office. It was good to know he hadn't lost his touch with the women. If Brianna weren't in the picture, he would have bedded Lisa the first time she'd flirted with him. He had no issue with a woman going after what she wanted. From the looks of things, Lisa wanted him and wanted him bad.

After dinner, Lisa turned on the radio and tuned it to his favorite jazz station. "Would you like anything else to drink?" she asked.

Jake placed his hand over the top of his glass. "I've had enough. I can't be drunk and driving."

"We can settle that. You can just stay here," Lisa said as she let the wrap dress she wore open up, exposing her body, which was draped in see-through black lace underwear. Lisa didn't wait for Jake to confirm or deny his attraction. She pounced on him and soon had him in a lip-locking session.

Jake's body yearned for a woman's touch. He loved Brianna, and the thought of her caused his erection to deflate. Lisa's phone rang. She stopped and answered it. Jake felt relief. He would have been embarrassed if she had seen he couldn't get it up.

"Too late. It's a done deal," Lisa said to whomever she was speaking with. She continued going back and forth for a few minutes. She finally hung up the phone. "Where were we?"

Jake wiped the red lipstick from his lips. "Sounds like that's something you really need to take care."

"That was a client who wanted to renege on a deal."

"The phone call saved me. Saved us from doing something we both would regret later." Jake grabbed his jacket and rushed out before his body did cooperate and he did something he would regret—like cheating on Brianna.

CHAPTER 41

"No, no, no," Brianna screamed out loud. How could she have handed Jake over to another woman? Jake was hers. In spite of their issues, he was hers, and now he was sleeping with her friend. Correction, her ex-friend. She had called Lisa to tell her she had changed her mind, and Lisa had acted like she didn't care. She had called Lisa several times afterward, and the heifer had refused to answer her phone.

Brianna grabbed her purse and bumped into Jake as she ran out the front door. "What are you doing here?" she cried.

"I live here. Where are you going in such a hurry?"

Brianna didn't know if she should hug him for being there or slap him for sleeping with Lisa. She did neither. "I got to go."

She rushed out, leaving Jake standing in the doorway. She needed to see for herself. Hidden cameras had been planted in various places in the condo. She needed the tapes for proof. She also wanted to catch Lisa so she could kick her behind for sleeping with her man even after she had told her she'd changed her mind.

When she got to the condo, Lisa was long gone. She had left a disk and a note on the kitchen table. "Watch at your convenience."

Brianna's nerves couldn't take the suspense, so she placed the disk in the DVD player in the living room and waited. Lisa popped up on the screen. "You're a lucky woman. Jake is really one of the good guys. Sorry I couldn't have been of more help. P.S. The next time you devise a hare-brained scheme like this, don't call me. I'm out." The screen faded to a hazy gray.

"Yes," she screamed. She relaxed, knowing Jake hadn't gone through with it and had passed the test. She was her own worst enemy, it seemed.

She dialed Jake's cell phone. "I'm exhausted, so I'll be staying at my friend's house tonight."

"Do you want me to come get you?" he asked.

"No. I'll be fine. I'll see you tomorrow."

They said their good-byes. She had the condo for the entire weekend, so she might as well enjoy one night. She could tell Lisa had put the money she'd given her to good use. It looked like they had eaten well. She found some strawberries in the refrigerator. She washed a few off and ate them, then poured herself several glasses of wine. With the soft music playing in the background, she fell asleep on the couch.

It was late afternoon by the time Brianna made it home. She had showered at the condo earlier, but because she hadn't had a change of clothes, she'd made a detour to the mall before going to her hair appointment. She had decided to get a manicure and pedicure for the full pampering effect.

"Jake, I'm home," she yelled.

He didn't respond.

Her cell phone rang. "Hi, Lisa . . . yes. I got the video . . . I was very upset. You led me to believe you two slept together . . . No, I haven't talked to Jake. It's not like he's going to admit he almost slept with you."

Brianna turned around just in time to see the bouquet of flowers fall from Jake's hand to the floor. "Lisa, I have to go. Jake, I can explain."

"I think you've said enough," he snarled. He stormed out of the house.

Brianna rushed to the door. "Jake," she yelled several times as he jumped in his Jaguar and sped away.

Brianna went back into the house and paced the floor. She dialed his cell phone number, but to no avail. Each call went to voice mail. She had never wanted Jake to find out. How could she explain herself if he wouldn't talk to her? Her nerves were on edge. She called Tosha, but she wouldn't pick up her phone, either.

"Trent. What's Trent's number?" She went to Jake's office and opened up his phone book. She dialed Trent's number. When he picked up, she blurted, "Trent, I know we're not the best of friends, but if Jake calls you or stops by, please call me."

"I have to respect my boy's wishes. If he doesn't want to talk to you, I can't be going behind his back."

"Please. I just need to make sure he's okay. I can't tell you what happened, but I'm sorry, and I really need for him to know that."

Trent placed her on hold. "That's him now."

"Let me talk to him."

"It's best if you just let him cool down. You two can talk when he gets back home." Trent hung the phone up.

Brianna wasn't sure if she could depend on Trent. He was Jake's friend, not hers, anyway. The guilt was eating her up. She wasn't supposed to care this much. She hadn't planned on falling in love and getting a conscience. Brianna hoped Jake never found out about the things she had done that had affected his business. If he did, would their relationship be able to survive?

CHAPTER 42

Jake recounted what had happened with Lisa. Trent listened in disbelief when Jake said, "Man, Brianna was setting me up. If I had slept with Lisa, that would have been a wrap."

"I have to hand it to your girl. She's a slick one."

"I thought I could trust her. I thought we were past the contract and were really exploring our feelings."

Trent interrupted him. "Never trust a woman when it comes to money."

"I'm so pissed right now, you just don't know. I'm dealing with trying to get my son, and Brianna pulls this mess."

"Calm down. Just go home and talk to her. It might not be what you think."

"I know what I heard."

"You're welcome to stay in the guest room."

Jake thought about it for a few seconds. "No, man, I'm sleeping in my own bed. I'm not letting Bri drive me from my home."

Talking to Trent calmed him down enough to return home. The light was on in the living room.

He tiptoed inside and watched Brianna as she slept on the couch. *How could someone look so innocent but be so conniving?*

Jake had planned on confessing the incident with Lisa to Brianna, but when he'd overheard Brianna's conversation, his feet wouldn't move. His mouth had gone dry. He'd opened it to say something, but he'd been so shocked to hear Brianna had set him up. The setup had almost worked, but his mind and body wouldn't agree to it. Why? Because she had crept into his mind and was a part of his heart. Guilt hadn't let him do it. Now he wished he would have gone through with it. It would have served her right. Then again, he would have lost his business, because he would have forfeited the rest of the inheritance money.

Maybe Brianna's doubts were right. Maybe all they had between them was a business deal. She couldn't be trusted, and after this incident, he was sure, she felt the same way about him. Her friend had probably filled her head with lies.

Jake pulled a blanket out of the downstairs closet and covered Brianna with it. He was mad at her, but her actions were a wake-up call. He needed to keep his feelings under control, or else he would be living in the poorhouse, and so would the hundreds of employees who depended on him. Jake had a son to get, so for the sake of his company and his son, he would do whatever he had to do to get along with Brianna, but his heart was officially on vacation. He headed upstairs to bed.

"What's this?" Jake asked out loud. He stooped to pick up a small notebook on the floor in the hallway outside of Brianna's room. Curiosity got the best of him. He thumbed through it. He saw his name written on the last several pages. He skimmed the pages. *So she does feel guilty, but most importantly, she loves me.*

"Give me that," Brianna said, snatching the notebook from his hands. "How dare you read my journal!"

Jake stuttered, "I . . . didn't realize . . . I found it right here, in the hallway."

She hugged the notebook tight. "We're even. You think I can't be trusted, and now I think you can't be trusted."

As much as Jake wanted to disagree, he couldn't. After the stunt she had pulled with Lisa, he couldn't let his guard down around her, but he also couldn't go on without addressing what she had done. "Let's go back downstairs, because we need to talk."

Brianna snapped, "We can talk right here." She entered her room and sat on the edge of her bed.

He followed her and sat on the other end. "If you meant what you said in your journal, we might be able to get past all of this."

"I meant it, but I don't regret doing what I did."

"Enough with the lies, Bri. You love me and I love you, too, so let's stop playing these silly games."

Brianna wouldn't look him in the eyes. He took his hand and gently touched her face, moving it in his direction. "Look at me," he said.

"I can't," Brianna responded.

"Bri, I'm putting my pride to the side. I need you. Tell me you need me, too." By now Jake's hands were in his lap.

Brianna turned her back to him and didn't say

a word. Jake stood and walked out of the room. He not only left Brianna alone in the room, but he left a piece of his heart.

The next few weeks went by in a blur. Jake poured himself into his job. Brianna became what he had dreaded—his invisible wife. They avoided each other as much as possible.

Jake was miserable, and the only solace he got was when he was wheeling and dealing in the office. The research and development department came up with a new product that would be tested in the market. If successful, his stock would be worth double, maybe even triple. Business was better than he had hoped. Too bad he couldn't say the same thing about his personal life.

One afternoon Overton called Jake and said, "We have a court date. I know it's last minute, but I need you and Brianna to meet me at the courthouse tomorrow morning. Otherwise, it'll be two more months before we can get on the docket."

Jake responded, "We'll be there." He hung up with Overton and wondered how he was going to mend things with Brianna between now and tomorrow. She could be mad at him, but would she destroy his chances of getting his son?

CHAPTER 43

"Oooh, you look like crap," Tosha said as she walked into Brianna's office and sat down in the chair across from her desk.

"It's been a rough couple of weeks." Brianna stopped typing and turned her chair around.

"A few of us are going to happy hour after work. You're welcome to join us."

"I'll pass. Work has me swamped."

Tosha picked through the candy jar until she found a piece of candy she wanted. "If I were the boss's wife, I wouldn't even be worried about it."

"Things aren't going great on the home front right now," Brianna admitted.

"You know helping folks with their relationships is my expertise, although why they want to listen to someone whose longest relationship was six months is beyond me. But, anyway, let Tosha help you." Tosha went on and on.

Brianna chuckled. "It's something I have to deal with, but thanks for the offer, girl."

"You sure? I have a good track record. I've saved several marriages."

Brianna grabbed her notepad and stood up. "Girl, I have a meeting to go to. Jake and I will be fine." She said it more to convince herself than Tosha.

Brianna arrived at the meeting early. Jake stood with his back facing the door. Brianna cleared her throat. Jake turned around. They both said at the same time, "We need to talk."

They laughed around each other for the first time in quite a while. "I'm not sure this is a good time," Brianna said.

"I cancelled the meeting with everybody else. It's just the two of us." Jake walked to the door, shut it, and locked it.

Brianna leaned on the table. "Here we are."

Jake walked toward her and stopped right in front of her. "You and me."

The tension from the past few weeks seemed to subside as soon as Jake's lips covered Brianna's.

"I'm sorry," Brianna admitted when she came up for air. She was now sitting on top of the table, and Jake stood in between her legs.

"It's been hard living under the same roof with you and not being able to touch you and talk to you," Jake said.

"We've talked."

"Small talk doesn't count." Jake kissed her on the forehead, then sat down in a nearby chair. "I need to discuss something serious with you."

Brianna remained sitting on the edge of the table. "Is it about the business?"

"No. Business is good. It's about my son. My lawyer has a court date set up for me to try to get him."

"Jake, that's great news."

"I know we haven't talked much about the situation, but I'll need you to go to court with me in the morning. We need to put on a united front."

"So trying to make up is about your kid. It isn't about making amends at all, is it?" Brianna snapped.

"It isn't just about Christopher."

"Whatever, Jake." Brianna slid off the table and almost tumbled. Jake caught her. She pushed his hands away.

"Bri, please," Jake pleaded.

"I'll think about it." Brianna swore she saw a few tears in Jake's eyes, and that was what stopped her from leaving the room. She hadn't seen him like this before. She didn't have the heart to resist him. "Fine. What do I need to do?"

"You may get asked a few questions, but other than that, you being there will be enough."

Later that night, Jake surprised Brianna with a candlelight dinner. Brianna broke the ice by saying, "Jake, I want to apologize again for the situation with Lisa."

"I think I was disappointed more than anything. I thought you were finally trusting me, so it hurt," Jake admitted.

Brianna washed her food down with her drink. "I love you, but after Byron cheated on me, trusting a man hasn't been easy for me to do."

"Haven't I proven to you that I can be trusted?"

Brianna thought about her original plans of revenge, although she had given up those plans long ago. Could she trust Jake? She responded, "Jake, so far, you have shown me you can be trusted."

"Can we start sharing a bed again? I would love

to be able to tell Betty to move all your stuff to my room. I mean our room."

Brianna thought about it for a moment. "Sure, we're married, and married folks should sleep in the same bed."

They sealed their agreement with a long night of lovemaking.

CHAPTER 44

Jake woke up before Brianna. He brushed the hair from her forehead as she slept. He didn't want to move but knew they would need to get up and get dressed so they wouldn't be late for court. He gently shook Brianna. "Time to get up, Sleeping Beauty," he said and planted a kiss on her lips.

Brianna stirred. "I have morning breath, so you might want to save the kisses."

He kissed her again. "We have an hour to get ready, so get up." Jake left Brianna stretching in bed. He went to his closet to locate his favorite navy blue suit.

Less than an hour later, Brianna stood at the end of the stairway, dressed in a pin-striped navy blue dress suit. Her hair was pulled back in a bun, with a few ringlets of hair falling on the sides. She extended her hand out, and he took it as they walked out the door to head to court.

The Dallas traffic didn't disappoint. Despite being stuck in traffic, they made it to the courthouse with ten minutes to spare. Overton was waiting for them outside the courtroom. "I was just about to call you," he said. He extended his hand out to Brianna. "Mrs. Banks, thanks for coming. Jake's going to need you."

"I wouldn't have missed it," Brianna responded.

"Follow me," Overton said. He led them to the front of the courtroom. Brianna took a seat first. Jake and Overton sat on the left side of her, closer to the aisle. "We'll sit here until our case is called. If either one of you feels unsure about a question their attorney or the judge asks you, just say so and I'll have them clarify."

Jake reached over and placed his hand on top of Brianna's and squeezed it.

The bailiff said, "All rise. This court is now in session. The Honorable Judge Carrie Prudence is residing."

Judge Prudence said, "You may all be seated." She looked at some of the files in front of her. Jake watched as several people went before the judge. He hoped she had compassion when it came to his case. "Will Jacob Banks and Byron Matthews and their attorneys come forward?"

Jake heard Brianna gasp. "What's wrong?"

"He's my ex."

Jake followed Brianna's gaze. Byron Matthews, emaculately dressed in a black suit, held a woman's hand and walked toward the table on the right-hand side of the court, with a man who must have been his attorney. "I remember him. You danced with him at our reception."

Overton interrupted his train of thought. "Jake, come on. You're up."

Jake couldn't believe his luck. How could Brianna's ex be the man standing in the way of him having his son? They moved to a table closer to the judge. Jake stood in between Brianna and

Overton and sat only when directed to do so by the judge.

Overton approached the bench and handed the judge some information. Time stood still as she read over the information. She addressed Jake first. After he was sworn in, she asked, "Mr. Banks, is it true that you didn't know Christopher Matthews was your biological son?"

"Yes, Your Honor. Tara Spain provided me with a false DNA report."

The judge wrote down a few notes as he spoke. She continued to ask questions. "Can you tell the court how you learned of the false report?"

"I was informed by my attorney. He learned of it while doing research for my late uncle, Jack Banks," replied Jake.

"Your Honor, how do we know this research is accurate? It's already been established that Tara Spain was a liar," said Byron Matthews's attorney.

"With all due respect, Your Honor and Ms. Williams," Overton said, addressing the other attorney. "A second set of tests has been done per court orders, and the results confirmed that Jacob Banks is Christopher's father. We are petitioning for custody of his son."

The woman sitting next to Byron whispered in his attorney's ear. Ms. Williams stood and said, "My client would like to appeal to the court. Christopher has known only Byron and Nicolette Matthews as his mom and dad for the past three years of his life. Taking him away from a structured and loving home could be detrimental to his mental well-being." Ms. Williams cited examples of how moving Christopher from one household to another might pose issues for him in the long run.

Jake hadn't thought of it that way before. He whispered to Brianna, "What do you think?"

"You seem to love the child—sight unseen—so don't let them play mind games with you," she responded.

Overton turned to face him. "I'm not sure how you feel, but would you agree to joint custody?"

"I don't want to disrupt his life in a way that will scar him. But he needs to know that I love him, and I want to be a part of his life. I don't want him to have to grow up without a father, like I did."

Brianna squeezed Jake's hand for support. "Whatever you decide, I'm behind you one hundred percent," she assured him.

Jake whispered in Overton's ear.

"Mr. Overton, have you and your client decided how you would like to proceed?" Judge Prudence asked.

Overton responded, "Judge Prudence, my client, Mr. Banks, and his wife, Brianna, would like full custody."

"I object," Ms. Williams shouted.

Overton continued. "I wasn't finished. However, knowing that Christopher has grown up in a stable and loving home, as Ms. Williams has pointed out, we feel that it is in the child's best interest to grow up with two sets of parents. We are hereby asking for joint custody."

Byron and Nicolette didn't seem too thrilled by this request. Ms. Williams stood up. "My clients would like some time to think about this, Your Honor."

Judge Prudence said, "Your clients have had a few months to think about this. I think it's an unselfish decision on Mr. Banks's part. He was not

aware that he was a father, and he could have ignored the fact. Instead, he took the initiative to
become a part of Christopher's life. Since he is
saving the court time by not having us go back
and forth on this issue, I would like for your
clients to reconsider and agree to his offer for
joint custody. You will have until the end of the
month to decide. In the meantime, I advise you to
get with your clients and come up with a schedule
for Mr. Banks and his wife to meet Christopher.
The first few visits should be supervised by Mr.
Matthews or Mrs. Matthews. It will be a transition,
but I'm confident that with two sets of parents,
Christopher will grow up knowing that he's loved,
and that makes him one lucky fellow."

"Thank you," Jake said out loud, looking up
toward heaven.

Judge Prudence's gavel sounded. "You all can
meet in my chambers. Court is adjourned until
one o'clock."

CHAPTER 45

Brianna hoped her weak knees didn't give out on her as she followed everyone to the judge's chambers. She still couldn't get over the fact that her ex-boyfriend was Jake's son's adopted father. She took a seat next to Jake.

Overton and Byron's attorney spoke to each other. Overton then addressed Brianna and Jake. "We're going to leave you all to talk among yourselves. We'll be back shortly."

Byron and Nicolette sat directly across from her and Jake. Jake held her hand under the table. Brianna could tell Jake was uncomfortable. She decided to be the one to break the silence. "Byron, I don't think you've introduced me to your wife."

Byron shifted in his seat. Nicolette had her arms folded. "Nikki, this is Brianna. The one I told you about," Byron said.

Nicolette uncrossed her arms. "You left out one thing. She is Christopher's biological dad's wife."

Jake interrupted and said, "You two will have

to discuss that later. We're supposed to be talking about my son."

Nicolette addressed Jake. "Excuse me if I'm not too thrilled by this arrangement."

"Nikki. I can call you Nikki, can't I? It's not Jake's fault. Let's work together, because it seems we're going to be an extended family," Brianna said.

Byron said, "Bri is right. We have to be civil to each other. Jake, you and Brianna can come over to see Christopher this Saturday."

"I don't think Saturday's a good time. How about Sunday?" Nicolette asked.

Jake looked at Brianna before responding. "Saturday works best for us."

Byron whispered something in Nicolette's ear. Nicolette said, "Saturday's fine. It'll have to be late, though. Come over around six."

Brianna said, "Great. Give us your address, and we'll be there."

Brianna and Jake walked to the car in silence. Jake opened her door. Once they were on the freeway, Jake said, "Thank you for having my back. It really means a lot."

She let out a sigh of relief. The past few hours had felt surreal. "I don't think I like Nikki. She seemed to have an attitude problem."

"We have to look at it like this. She probably feels threatened. She thinks we're going to take her child away."

"That's stupid, because we agreed to joint custody, so she needs to chill with the attitude."

"Wow, you're really taking this custody thing serious."

"Well, yes. I'm going to be a mother now, so I have to." Brianna stopped in mid-thought. It dawned on her at that moment, she was about to be some child's role model.

"I remember seeing you dance with Byron Matthews at the reception. Did he mention anything about Christopher then?" Jake asked.

"Of course not. We barely talked."

"It seemed like a lot of talking was going on to me."

"If you must know, he was apologizing for hurting me. That was it. I was just as shocked as you were to see him in court today."

"Do you think you'll be able to handle being a mom to Christopher? If not, let me know now, because I don't want him to get attached to you and you to leave us. I mean him," Jake said.

"Jake, I can only promise you I will do my best to love him as my own. Everything else depends on you."

Jake turned up the music, and they rode home, each thinking about the day's events. Once at home, Brianna escaped to the bathroom. She dialed Bridget's number. She didn't realize how emotional the situation was until Bridget answered. Before she knew it, she was crying on the phone.

"Bri, calm down. Do you need me to come over?" Bridget asked.

"No. I'm okay," Brianna said in between sniffles. She told Bridget about Christopher, what the judge had ordered, and Jake's responses.

"Are you really ready to be someone's mom?"

"I have no choice."

"Oh, you have a choice. At the end of the year,

you can go your way and leave Jake with his son," Bridget said.

"I love Jake."

"Then do whatever you need to do and pull yourself together. A child senses things. If you're going to be a part of the child's life, you need to get a grip on your emotions."

CHAPTER 46

Jake followed Brianna from one store to the next as she took him on a shopping spree for Christopher. "I don't know what he likes, but if we get a little bit of everything—"

"Whoa! Slow down, Bri. You're more excited about all of this than I am." Jake grabbed her arm.

"I need to get a few books. I have no clue on how to be a mom," she said.

"We'll both be winging it," he said as he took the bags away from Brianna.

Two hours later, they pulled up in front of the Matthews' house. "Do you want me to wait here?" asked Brianna.

"Come on. You're going in, too."

Jake opened her car door. Hand in hand, they walked to the front door. Jake rang the doorbell. They waited a few minutes before the door opened. Byron, casually dressed, greeted them. "Come on in."

Brianna walked through the door, with Jake following close behind. "You have a nice place," Brianna commented.

"Thanks. Chris and Nikki are in the den," said Byron.

Jake looked around as they followed Byron. His heart skipped a beat at the sight of a healthy three-year-old playing with Nicolette. Christopher looked in their direction and said, "Daddy."

Jake's heart dropped, knowing those words were meant for Byron and not him. Byron bent over to pick Christopher up. "Li'l man, I want you to meet someone." Christopher seemed to hug Byron tightly.

"Hello, Chris," Jake said, picking up on the name from Byron's initial conversation.

Nicolette stood by Byron's side. "Say hello to Jake and Brianna."

"Hew-o."

"Can I hold him?" Jake asked.

Byron attempted to hand Christopher to Jake, but he wouldn't let go of Byron's shirt.

Nicolette said, "He's like that with strangers."

"Give him a little time," Byron suggested.

Brianna reached for him, and Christopher went to her without any problems. Byron looked up. "Hey, she's a woman. Can't blame the child."

Jake and Byron laughed. Nicolette rolled her eyes. "Be careful. He doesn't like to be held too tight."

Brianna tickled him. "I know a little about kids."

"Each child is different," Nicolette snapped.

Brianna found a seat and held Christopher. Jake sat next to her. After about fifteen minutes, Christopher felt comfortable letting Jake hold him. Jake couldn't explain the feeling that engulfed his entire being when he held Christopher in his arms. He closed his eyes and inhaled the boy's scent. He wanted to remember this moment for the rest of his life.

Byron said, "Chris, you're a lucky little boy. You have two daddies and two mommies."

Christopher said, "Da-da."

Jake said, "That's right. I'm your daddy, too. I love you so much."

"I love ooh," Christopher repeated.

Joy filled Jake's heart.

Christopher said, "Pot-pot."

"Come on, Chris. Let's go." Byron picked up Christopher.

"He's potty trained already?" Brianna asked.

Nicolette said, "Yes, he's a quick learner."

Jake could feel the tension between the two women. "Nikki, thank you for letting us see Chris today."

Nicolette looked in the direction Byron and Christopher had just gone and then turned around to look at him and Brianna. "This isn't easy for me."

"We understand," Jake said.

Nicolette sat in the love seat across from the sofa. "No, I don't think you do. I didn't like Tara—"

"I didn't know her, and I don't like her," Brianna interrupted.

"Trust me, you're better off not knowing her," replied Nicolette.

"Ladies, it's not polite to talk ill of the dead," Jake interjected.

They both looked at him and rolled their eyes.

Nicolette said, "I apologize to you both for coming across as kind of harsh, but I love that little man in there, and I just can't imagine my life without him."

"We have no plans to take him away," Jake assured her. "Want what's best for him, and I can tell you guys love him very much."

"We do. Oh, where was I? Tara, as Jake should know, was a character. She did her best to break up Byron and me. When she died—God forgive me for saying this—I was glad she wouldn't be a thorn in our side anymore. We had no idea who Christopher's biological father was, but we didn't want him going into the system."

"I appreciate that, because I might not have ever gotten to know him if he had," said Jake.

"We tried to find you," Nicolette admitted, "We didn't know your name, but we had an investigator look for his real father. Once we hit a dead end, Byron and I decided to adopt him and make him officially ours."

Jake's face lit up when Christopher walked into the room. He tuned out everything else as he spent time with his son. Brianna was unusually quiet. He wondered how she felt about their first encounter. He would soon find out.

CHAPTER 47

"While you were playing with Chris, Nikki told me she was planning a huge birthday party for his fourth birthday," Brianna said as she curled her legs under her while sitting on their couch.

"It's a little early to be doing that, don't you think?" Jake asked as he reached for a slice of pizza.

"His birthday is a few months away, but you have to look at it like this. At least she's including us in the planning phase."

"So what do you think about Chris?" Jake asked.

"I think he's a bright little boy who is as cute as his daddy," Brianna responded.

"I thought he wasn't going to take to me for a minute."

"Give him some time."

"It went better than I thought it would. He did call me daddy."

"No, he said 'Da-da'," Brianna teased.

"I'm proud of how you kept your cool with Byron and Nikki."

"Byron and I are history. You and Christopher are my future."

"True." Jake yawned. "I don't know about you, but I'm sleepy."

"Go on up. I'll clean up down here," Brianna said.

Jake kissed her on the lips and left her downstairs.

The end of the month came fast. Jake called Brianna into his office. "I just got word from Overton, and it's official. All parties have signed. We have joint custody."

Brianna sat in Jake's lap. "Congrats, Daddy."

"That's Big Daddy to you," Jake said as he kissed her.

Joan entered the office and alerted them to her arrival by clearing her throat. "Sorry. I didn't mean to interrupt."

Brianna jumped up. She smoothed out the wrinkles in her skirt. "I have a conference call I'm late for. Jake, see you at home. Bye, Joan," she said as she passed the smiling secretary.

"Mrs. Banks, can I see you for a moment?" one of the IT employees said as Brianna exited the elevator on her floor.

"What can I help you with?"

"It's something I need to show you. But in private."

Brianna looked at the employee's name tag. It read VICTOR HAGON.

She led him to her office. "Victor, can it wait? I have a conference call."

"It'll only take a few minutes of your time."

Once they were in her office, he handed her a

folder with the words VENDOR DISCREPANCY REPORT displayed on the label. Victor said, "I have you down as the point of contact if we found any discrepancies."

"Yes." Brianna wasn't sure if she was ready to hear more.

"We found several entries where it appears a hacker made transactions on accounts under your log-in."

Brianna's past transgressions were now haunting her. She played it off. "Give me some time to look through this, and I'll get back with you."

"I wasn't sure if you wanted to handle it directly or give it to someone else."

Brianna said, "I'll look these over, and if need be, I'll talk to Mr. Banks."

As soon as Victor left her office, she closed her door. She decided not to call into the conference. She had more immediate things to take care of—like figuring out how to make sure Jake never saw the information that could prove she was behind several projects failing. She threw the folder in her laptop case. She sent out a message to her staff to let them know she was leaving early, logged off her computer, and unhooked her laptop.

Tosha exited the elevator as Brianna was getting on. "Girl, you look like someone's after you."

"I'm not feeling well, so I'm on my way home."

"Do you need me to drive you?"

Brianna held up her hand. "No. I just need a nap, and I'll be fine."

She hit the close button on the elevator and didn't wait for Tosha to respond. She paced the floor of the elevator. When she reached the lobby, she walked briskly past the security desk without saying a word. It seemed to her that she didn't release her breath until she was sitting on the highway, far away from Banks Telecom.

"Bridget, my past has caught up with me," Brianna said as soon as her sister answered the door.

"Come on in."

Brianna showed her the folder. Bridget skimmed it. "Tell Jake."

"He wouldn't understand. It took us months to get to this point."

"I'm the first to admit, Jake hasn't been my favorite person, but he makes you happy."

"I'm not meant to be happy. I'm convinced of that now," Brianna said, accepting defeat.

"This happened at a different time in your life. You gave up your quest for revenge months ago."

"But Jake's not going to see that. He's going to blame me for his company's previous hardships."

"We all make mistakes," Bridget said.

"Some mistakes are easier to forgive than others."

CHAPTER 48

Spending time with his son over the past few weeks had Jake in a jovial mood, but something was amiss concerning Brianna. When she didn't think he was paying attention, she would sometimes have a faraway look in her eyes. Jake ignored it as long as he could.

"Bri, I want to know what's going on with you, and I want to know now," he demanded when he burst into her office.

Brianna wasn't there. He sat down behind her desk to wait for her. While sitting and waiting, he decided to write her a note. He didn't see a pen, so he attempted to open up the top desk drawer. It was locked. He looked in her laptop case for a key. A folder in the case caught his attention. He pulled it out. He recalled the argument that had ensued the last time he got caught snooping. He pushed the thought to the side and looked in the folder.

He couldn't believe what he was seeing. The accounts listed in the folder were the same ones that had led to him losing money. He forgot about leaving her a note. He took the folder with him and headed to his office.

"Joan, do me a favor and cancel all my meetings for the rest of the day," he said as he passed his secretary's desk.

Jake locked his door and took the time to go through the details in the folder thoroughly. Each one of the accounts showed Brianna had been the one to enter in the figures. He had one question. Why? Why had Brianna tried to sabotage his company? All this time, he had been sleeping with the enemy.

Jake left the office and spent the afternoon figuring out how he would confront Brianna. It took all the restraint he had not to go to her office again. This was something he needed to handle in private. If his temper flared, he didn't want it to happen around his employees.

Brianna turned the lock on the door and yelled out, "Sorry, I'm late. I stopped at the store to pick up a few things for Chris's room."

Jake didn't respond. Brianna called out his name a few times. "Jake, are you downstairs? You must be upstairs."

Jake yelled, "No, I'm downstairs. I'm in the living room."

"See what I got." Brianna stopped talking when she saw the anger on Jake's face. "What's wrong? Are Nikki and Byron tripping about Chris?"

Jake threw the folder at her, and papers started flying everywhere. "What the hell is your problem?" Brianna asked as she stooped down to retrieve the papers. She stopped when she realized what they were. "Jake, I . . . I can explain," she stuttered.

"I trusted you. I trusted you with my life, with my child, and you betrayed me."

"It's not what you think." Brianna walked up to him. "This all happened before I knew you."

"You were working at my company. You knew me quite well."

"No. It was before we really got to know each other. You just don't understand the pressure I was under."

Brianna reached out to him, but he blocked her efforts by folding his arms. "Pressure? Let me explain to you about pressure. What you did put my whole company at risk! Do you know what would have happened if my uncle hadn't left me the money? Do you? People would have been out of jobs. Whole families would have been affected by something that you set in motion."

"I didn't think about that when I set out to get revenge."

"Bri, what did I ever do to you? My company offered you a job. Grant it, our relationship wasn't conventional, but I showed you love, and I thought you loved me."

"I do love you, Jake. The revenge was set in motion when my dad died."

"What does your dad have to do with me?"

"Your uncle turned down my dad for a loan. When he did, it set off a chain of events that led my father into a deep depression. He never fully recovered from it, and when he died, something inside of me died along with him. Getting revenge on your uncle was how I got the strength to go on. Please understand."

"I understand one thing, Bri. You're not the woman I thought you were."

"Jake, we can work through this. We got through the Lisa thing. We got through the Christopher thing."

"Don't you say another thing about my son. If he wasn't so taken with you, I would ban you from seeing him."

"Jake, I never meant to hurt you. I wanted to hurt your uncle Jack," Brianna said.

"When Uncle Jack died, your quest for revenge should have died right along with him, but it didn't."

Brianna said, "I did let it go."

"But not soon enough. I suggest you sleep in the guest room. Your stuff's already been moved to it."

Jake's heart ached as he watched Brianna leave the room. Her betrayal had pierced his heart. Jake would find a way to ride out the next few months until the year was up. Brianna would be his wife in name only; as far as he was concerned, she would be invisible.

IV

TIME FLIES WHEN YOU'RE HAVING FUN

CHAPTER 49

Jake and Brianna's one-year anniversary was approaching. Jake made a phone call to Overton to discuss his uncle's will. Overton confirmed that no matter if his marriage was working or not, the remainder of the funds would be relinquished to him without any other stipulations once the one year had passed.

A few hours later, a courier brought over some documents from Overton. Jake didn't have any other appointments scheduled, so he locked his office door so he could review the documents in private. Included in the documents was a letter from his uncle Jack, as well as other papers he would need to review before approaching Brianna to discuss their divorce.

Divorce. He had never thought he would seek one. Actually, he had never thought he would say the words *I do* either, but he had. He still loved Brianna, but since their blowup after he found out about her misdeeds, they had both kept their distance as much as possible. He had forgiven her, but he couldn't forget what she had done.

They had been cordial to each other over the past few months. She had attended events with him when he needed an escort, but he had barely seen her dimples. It seemed like he took the life out of her when he was around. He missed the Brianna that put up a fight whenever he challenged her; he wasn't used to the Brianna who seemed compliant. The only time she seemed happy was when Christopher was around. He didn't look forward to the day Brianna would be out of their lives.

"Let's see what dear old Uncle Jack had to say," Jake said out loud.

> *Jake, if you're reading this, it means I've gone on to glory. I love you. It hurt me that you had to grow up without your parents, but the Lord saw fit to bring you into our lives. Me and your aunt loved you and couldn't have asked for a better nephew, or, I should say, son. I want you to know I'm so proud of you. I wanted you to go into banking, but we're too much alike. You wanted to be your own man. To build a company from scratch is hard, but by golly, you got those strong Banks genes, and you did it. My son, Jacob Banks, the CEO of his own company. By now you've probably said a few unkind words about me, but I forgive you.*
>
> *There are two versions of this letter. The other version says the same thing but congratulates you. If you're reading this letter, it means you and Brianna couldn't make things work during this past year. I'm sorry it didn't work out. I hope it's not because you were reunited with your son. I regret I never got a chance to meet Christopher. I've set aside money to be given to him on his twenty-first birthday.*
>
> *Brianna has the same passion as your aunt. Son, you need a helpmate—one who will love*

*you for you and not for what you can do for her.
Brianna is that woman, so whatever it is you have
to work through, don't let her get away.*

*She and her siblings have every right to blame
me—and that they did. I forgave their father. You
forgive them. If you love her, go after her. Go after
her the same way you went after her to save your
business. You didn't hesitate to approach her when
it came to saving your business, so save your heart
and go after the woman you love. I don't want you
to be alone. You need someone to love you and care
for you, because I'm no longer there. I love you, son.*

The letter fell out of his hands as he wiped the
tears from his eyes. Here he was, a grown man,
crying. He had to pull himself together. His uncle
had included several tidbits of information he
would have to check out. He thought about the
hostility Brianna sometimes showed toward him
for no apparent reason. Jake leaned his head
back as he thought about how to proceed. Brianna. The Mayfields. Uncle Jack. So many questions ran through his mind. Love tugged at his
heart.

CHAPTER 50

Brianna marked the days off on her calendar. Time was running out. She and Jake had been going through the motions. He was like the silent roommate. They communicated in passing, whenever he had an event that required an escort, or to put up a united front in front of Byron and Nikki. Otherwise, they were like two ships passing in the night.

Brianna poured herself into her work, but she was tired of dealing with coworkers and subordinates who saw her as Mrs. Banks and didn't accept the fact she was good at her job. Brianna was lucky Jake had let her keep her job after he found out what she'd done. Brianna dreaded leaving Jake, but with their one-year anniversary approaching, she knew it was inevitable. She planned on taking a portion of the money Jake would give her and starting her own consulting firm.

Brianna typed her resignation letter, removed it from the printer, and signed it. She walked the letter to Neil Franks, the vice president over her.

She handed him the letter and sat across from his desk.

Neil read the letter. "Does Jake know about this?" he asked.

"Neil, me resigning has nothing to do with Jake. I make my own decisions."

"I'll have to run this past him."

Brianna stood up. "It's a done deal. I'll have everything wrapped up in a week."

She was fuming. She knew leaving was the right thing to do. Her fate had been sealed the day she stepped foot inside Banks Telecom. Once she divorced Jake, she didn't want to have anything to do with him or his company. She would miss Christopher, but she would get over losing him, too. Continuing to work at Banks Telecom wouldn't be good for her emotionally or mentally. Since D-day, as she called the day she would sign the divorce papers, was getting closer, it was best that she moved on. Neither Neil nor Jake would be able to change her mind.

By the time Brianna reached her office, Jake was sitting behind her desk.

"No, you can't change my mind," Brianna blurted out, without giving him a chance to say anything.

"I came to tell you there's no need to wait two weeks. You can leave now."

"I need to go over some things with a few people in my department."

He interrupted her. "No need to. You keep good notes. I'll have Diane or someone else take over."

Brianna should have been happy. She was getting what she wanted—an opportunity to start her own business. For that, she would always be thankful to the Banks. "If there isn't anything else, I need to pack up some of my things. I hadn't planned on leaving this early, but since you're giving me the boot—"

Jake stood up. "I'm not kicking you out. You're the one who decided to leave."

Why didn't it sound like he was talking about business? She ignored the desire to wrap her arms around his neck and kiss him. The twinkle she hadn't seen in his eyes in months had returned. Maybe her mind was playing tricks on her. Reality struck.

"I need a box or something," she rambled.

"I'll have someone pack your stuff. Why don't you call it a day?"

"I didn't want to leave like this. I need to tell my staff. I want to be the one to tell them."

"Okay. I'll give you twenty-four hours. I'll still have someone come move your stuff for you. Make an announcement by tomorrow morning, or else I will," Jake said before leaving the room.

His cologne lingered in the room. It wrapped itself around her like a hug. She closed her door and locked it. She didn't want to be disturbed the rest of the afternoon. She logged on to her e-mail program and sent out a department-wide announcement about an emergency meeting to be held the next morning.

Later that night, Brianna waited for Jake to show up at home so she could discuss her resignation. By ten he still hadn't shown up, so she gave up and retired to bed. It was after midnight when she heard Jake come up the stairs. She closed her eyes and fell asleep a short time afterward.

The next morning she dressed in a designer suit and took extra time to curl her hair. She wore her mother's pearl necklace and earrings set. She purposely arrived late to the conference room where her emergency meeting was being held. She wanted to make a grand entrance, and that she did. She stopped in mid-step when she saw Jake sitting at the back of the room.

"Thank you all for being here at such short notice. I wanted to let you all know I will be leaving Banks Telecom to start my own business. Today is my last day," announced Brianna. People mumbled, but she continued. "I've enjoyed working with each and every one of you. Unless someone has any questions, that's it."

Several people came up to congratulate her. Thirty minutes later the only two people left in the conference room were her and Jake. He made her nervous. What did he want? He had made her leave earlier than she had planned on. Did he enjoy seeing her sweat? He sat in the back and stared. She refused to say anything else to him. If he wanted to play the staring game, she was not going to oblige him. Soon they would be going their separate ways. She had consulted with an attorney, and soon she would be a free woman—free from Jake at the job and at home.

CHAPTER 51

Joan said, "Jake would like to see you in the big conference room on the seventh floor."

"I'll be there as soon as I finish packing," Brianna responded.

"I thought we hired someone to do the packing for you."

"I sent them away. I wanted to do it myself. I don't have that much stuff. Just a few personal items."

"I'll let him know you'll be there in ten minutes."

"Sounds good."

Brianna would miss Joan. She had never shown any signs of disrespect, unlike some of her other colleagues. She placed the rest of her items in the box. She logged off her laptop for the last time and placed everything in a corner. After she came from the conference room with Jake, she would be leaving Banks Telecom. The past two years had been an experience. Brianna had set out to get revenge on Jake, but things hadn't turned out exactly how she'd wanted them to. *What a difference a year makes.*

Brianna said her good-byes to a few people as she made her way to the conference room. A crowd yelled "Surprise!" as soon as she opened the door. Brianna was really surprised because she didn't expect to see balloons, flowers, gift bags, and a big, beautiful cake trimmed with purple roses sitting in the center of the table.

Jake walked up to her and kissed her on the cheek. "You didn't think we were letting you go without some fanfare, did you?"

Jake's show of affection shocked her. She cleared her throat. "I don't know what to say. You got me. You didn't have to," she said as she turned and looked at Jake.

Jake responded, "You deserve it."

Several people said, "Hear, hear!" They held up their glasses filled with punch and cheered.

The whole scene felt overwhelming. Brianna couldn't control the tears. She picked up a napkin and wiped her face. "This is so unexpected. I didn't think it would be this hard to move on," she said out loud.

"You could always change your mind," Jake said.

"Thank you all," she said, then looked at Jake. "Thank you for this. It's unexpected."

He squeezed her hand. "Those are the best kinds of surprises."

Brianna walked around the room and made sure she spoke with everyone in attendance, one-on-one. It was way past six by the time everyone had left the conference room. Once again she and Jake were the last two in the room. She started to clean up.

"Leave it. Someone will come clean this up later," Jake told her.

"But I don't like leaving a mess."

"You know I know. I live with you." He laughed.

"Oh yeah. You do know my obsession." She walked toward the door. "Well, I need a cart to carry this stuff out."

"I'll have someone put it all in my car. Don't worry about a thing."

"Well, this is it. I meant what I said. I will miss it here. Banks is a good company."

"I'll tell the boss. He'll be glad to hear one of his employees, well, ex-employees, say that."

"Jake, I'll miss . . . ." She stopped, paused, and looked into his eyes. "Never mind. Good-byes are hard. I'll see you later at home, right?"

"Sure. Bye, Bri."

She practically skipped to the elevator. Jake had called her Bri, and he hadn't done that in months. Maybe he was softening some. Then again, it had been an emotional day, so she wouldn't read more into it than was there.

Tosha was waiting outside her office door. "Girl, I'm going to miss you around here." She hugged her.

Brianna unlocked her door. "Have a seat," she said as she walked behind her desk and sat down in the chair.

"So what are your plans?"

"I'm starting my own business." Tosha didn't look like she believed her. "You act like this is the first time you've heard this. I've been talking about this forever."

Tosha sat on the corner of her desk. "But why now? You're married to one of the richest men in Dallas. You don't need to work. Still, you've been working, and now you're venturing off to start a new business, which will take up even more of your time. Some people have it good and don't even realize it."

"Believe me, you don't want to be walking in my shoes right about now. Besides, I've never depended on a man before, and I don't plan on starting now."

"Jake doesn't seem like the type that would let his woman want for anything. He threw you a nice going-away party—although rumor has it, he had no idea you were resigning."

Brianna laughed. "Tell the office gossip pool that no, he didn't know. He might be my husband, but he's not the boss of me. I can and do think for myself."

"I heard that," Tosha said. She picked up Brianna's desk calendar, which was still sitting on the desk, and flipped through it. "Do you need an assistant? You know for the right price, I might be available."

"When I do, you'll be the first person I call."

"So you and Jake have any special plans for tonight?" Tosha asked.

Brianna wished. The burden of the past year overpowered her. She needed to talk to someone. "Promise me something, Tosha."

"Uh-oh. Can I hear you out first before I answer?"

"No. Promise me you won't repeat what I'm about to tell you."

"Scouts' honor." Tosha held up two fingers.

"Jake and I are getting a divorce. Well, I think we are, anyway."

Tosha scooted farther back on the desk.

"What? Not the same Jake I saw give you loving looks less than an hour ago."

"Things haven't been too well at home, and the strain, well, the strain is getting to be too much. Too much for both of us."

"Whatever it is, you two need to work it out. You're good together. You can't break up. You're like Dallas's own Will and Jada. You're a powerhouse. Come on. Stay together. Do it for me. Do it for the single sisters who wish they had a black knight like Jake."

Brianna couldn't do anything but laugh at Tosha's dramatic behavior. After going back and forth with Tosha about relationships, she picked up her box and walked out of her office for the last time. She left the office that night, closing on one part of her life.

CHAPTER 52

Brianna thought that the extra two weeks she had to work on implementing her business plan would be productive, but they were far from it. She watched the calendar more than she did any work. In less than a month, it would be time for their one-year anniversary. Jake had been extra nice to her since she'd resigned from Banks Telecom. Maybe he was happy to get rid of her. She didn't know what to think. His actions seemed out of character. He had actually started acting like he had when they first got together.

He even got home early enough for them to at least say a few paragraphs to each other. She needed to be concentrating on her business instead of thinking about Jake. He invaded not only her dreams but her thoughts during the day. As soon as D-day—divorce day—came, maybe she could move on.

Brianna thought about her conversation with Tosha. Tosha seemed to be more concerned about the state of her marriage than she was. Tosha had e-mailed her tips on improving one's love life. Little did she know sex was not an issue—in fact, they weren't having it. Not that she didn't want to. Jake seemed to be getting finer and finer. Sometimes it seemed as if he purposely walked around with no shirt on so she could see his six-pack. His chest seemed to glisten, as if he had poured baby oil on it. Brianna fanned herself as she recalled the last time she saw Jake without his shirt on.

Brianna pulled the laptop on top of her lap and logged on to the Internet. Tosha had sent her several other relationship tips. She deleted each one of them, but not without reading them first. As much as she hated to admit it to herself, she wanted Jake. She didn't want their marriage to end. The hatred she had had in her heart for the Banks a year ago had turned into love, but soon Jake would be off-limits.

Brianna had some thinking to do. She needed to get away. She googled a few vacation spots. She opted for a four-day trip to the Bahamas. She made her reservations and logged off. Her cell phone rang. Bridget's name flashed across the screen.

"What's up, sis?"

She listened as Bridget described her dilemma. "I need someone to watch Danielle for a few days. If you do, I owe you one."

"Girl, please. Drop off my beautiful niece. Besides, it's time she and I got better acquainted."

An hour later, Bridget dropped off little Danielle Marie. She was as cute as a button and looked just like her auntie, or so Brianna claimed. "Thank you for doing this. Matt just found out about this trip, and you know he's trying to keep this job, We'll be gone one night, two tops," Bridget explained.

"Don't worry. Me and little Dani will be fine." Brianna played with the little girl's pacifier. "Besides, I can always call my new friend Nikki if I need some baby advice."

Bridget looked at her sideways. She kissed Danielle on the forehead. "Bye, baby. Mama promises to call you every hour. Don't give your auntie a hard time," Bridget said. "She likes to listen to music when she sleeps. Something soft, preferably jazz."

"Okay. Now go, before you miss your flight, and please, don't call me every hour."

Brianna played with Danielle until she fell asleep. Brianna went to clean up some and was surprised when she returned to the living room to see Jake holding Danielle. "She's so cute," he said as he rocked her in his arms.

"She was asleep," Brianna responded as she took the child from his arms and placed her back in the car seat.

"You look so cute holding her," he commented.

"Now that you're here, we'll just go upstairs so we won't be in your way."

"Don't go. She'll be just fine right here."

Brianna hesitated. She placed the car seat back near the couch. She watched Danielle fall asleep again. "I wish I could sleep that soundly."

"You and me both," Jake added. "How long will Danielle be with us?"

Brianna noticed he used the word *us* instead of *you*. "Bridget and Matt had to go out of town, so I agreed to watch her for a few days."

Danielle started crying. Jake beat Brianna to

the car seat. "No, let me," he said, then paused. "She just needs her diaper changed."

"Let me go get her diaper bag, and I'll change her."

"I got it. Bring me a diaper and her wipes. I'll be in the downstairs bedroom to the left."

Brianna stood there in disbelief for a minute. Okay, who was that man? Where was Jake? Christopher was in training pants, so how did Jake know anything about changing diapers? She went upstairs and retrieved the diaper bag. "Here's the diaper and the wipes. This I have to see. Mr. CEO changing a baby's diaper."

"Watch and learn. Watch and learn," he said as he changed Danielle's diaper. The child seemed to like Jake. He picked her up, and she smiled.

Jake handed her to Brianna, but Danielle wasn't having it. She started whining. "Traitor," Brianna teased.

"She loves her uncle Jake." He kissed Danielle on the cheek as she squirmed to get away from Brianna.

"Here. Take her. I'll go warm up her bottle."

"Do I sense some jealousy?" he asked as he cradled Danielle in his arms.

"You better be glad you're holding my niece, or I would pop you."

"Duly noted."

CHAPTER 53

Jake took the next day off to spend time with Brianna. He told her it was to help her out with Danielle. Christopher was there, too, so they were like one big, happy family. A delivery guy rang the doorbell. Jake signed for the package. It was addressed to Brianna and was from Destination Travels.

Danielle was sleeping in her car seat, and Christopher had fallen asleep on the love seat. Brianna sat on the couch, typing on her laptop. Jake handed Brianna the package. "So you're going on a trip?" he asked.

"To the Bahamas for a couple of days. You know, for a little R & R."

"When do you leave?"

"The day after Bridget and Matt return from their trip."

She pulled out the airline ticket and the brochures. Danielle started crying. Jake picked her up. "It's okay. Uncle Jake's here."

"You're spoiling her."

"That's what uncles are for."

Brianna smiled. "I thought I was bad. She has you wrapped around her little finger."

He tickled her. "She sure does. She can get anything she wants from Uncle Jake, just like her auntie."

Brianna didn't comment.

Jake didn't know who was more sad to see Danielle go, him, Brianna, or Christopher. He could tell Bridget and Matt had missed Danielle, because they practically ignored them when they stopped by to pick her up.

"Chris, we'll have to see if you can come visit Dani, okay, li'l man?" Matt said, picking him up and letting him get a closer look at Danielle.

"Anytime you need a babysitter, we're here," Jake said.

Brianna rolled her eyes at him. "She's a good baby. Auntie's going to miss you." Brianna tucked in her blanket.

Bridget hugged them both. "Well, we better get going. I don't like having her out in the night air."

"Thanks, man," Matt said, then shook Jake's hand. He hugged Brianna. "See you later, Bri."

Jake held Christopher as they all stood in the doorway, watching them leave. "Are you hungry?" he asked Brianna once they were gone.

"How about a hamburger?"

"Ham-urger," Christopher said.

"Two votes in. I'll throw a couple on the grill," said Jake.

"I'll chop up the lettuce and tomatoes."

Jake fired up his grill, and an hour later, they all sat around the kitchen table.

"Bri, these past few days have been great."

"Children will do it to you," she responded after taking a bite of her hamburger. He wiped her mouth with his napkin.

"Sorry, I couldn't resist."

"Jake, it's okay."

He felt like a shy teenager. He avoided eye contact. Watching Brianna and Christopher interact with one another tugged at his heart. Jake wanted more kids, and he wanted Brianna to be their mother. He no longer wanted the divorce.

"I'll get the dishes," Brianna volunteered when they were finished.

Christopher and Jake went to the living room. He picked up the travel brochure on the coffee table. He made a mental note of the hotel. He felt like going on a mini-vacation himself. Later that night, he went online and made plane reservations. He called the hotel and booked himself a room.

A few days later, Jake eyed the beautiful ocean water as his jet landed. By his watch, Brianna should be settled into her hotel. He had found out which room she was staying in at the Atlantis resort on Paradise Island and had booked the room right across from hers. He had to pay extra, but it would be well worth it.

Jake had slept on the plane, so he was well rested. Once he got settled in his room, he called Byron to check on Christopher. Not long afterward, he tried to get in contact with Brianna. She didn't answer after several tries. He showered and changed into something more befitting a vacation in the Bahamas and went in search of his woman—his wife.

The hotel lobby was crowded due to a convention, so Jake had his work cut out for him in locating Brianna. He paused for a moment. If he were Brianna, where would he be? He knew she loved shopping, so he passed by some of the shops in the mall portion of the resort.

He gave up on finding Brianna and decided to lounge on the beach. He bought a few items and went outside of the resort to find the perfect spot, preferably a spot with some shade. Jake heard her laughter before he saw Brianna's face.

He turned to see her grinning and laughing in the face of another man. His gray eyes darkened. *'So is this why she didn't invite me on her trip?'* he wondered.

CHAPTER 54

Brianna couldn't get Jake out of her mind no matter where she went. For a second, she thought she saw him standing near the entranceway to the aquarium. She blinked a few times, and he was gone. Her love for him had her hallucinating. She had taken this trip to get Jake out of her system, but it wasn't working. Seeing the couples made her wish she could enjoy moments like that with Jake.

Brianna removed the wrap, fully exposing her gold, two-piece swimsuit. She rubbed sunblock on her arms and legs and placed the big matching gold shades she had recently purchased over her eyes. She retrieved Michelle McGriff's latest thriller from her bag and spent the rest of the afternoon lounging on the beach and reading. She had planned on taking a nap, but the story kept her turning the pages. She finished the book just as the sun was going down.

McGriff's book had her looking over her shoulder. She became super aware of strangers as she walked back to the hotel. She wondered if any of them had done something as dangerous as some of the characters in the book she had just finished reading.

A beautiful array of flowers adorned the table in her room. She read the card and smiled. *I miss you. Love, J.*

Knowing Jake cared enough to send flowers made her day. She missed him, too. But reality stood between them. Their relationship had started because of a business deal, and it would end because of it. Brianna wanted Jake's love, but was it too late for them to make things work? She poured herself a glass of wine from the bar in her room. She held the glass up in the air. "Here's to a life without Jake."

An hour later, Brianna entered the hotel restaurant. "How many?" the maître d' asked.

"A table. . . ." Brianna didn't finish her statement.

"For two would be nice."

"Jake?"

"In the flesh. Thought I would join you for dinner."

They followed the maître d'. "You came all the way here to have dinner with me?" she asked.

"I got here this morning."

"But why didn't you tell me you were coming?"

"To have you change your plans? Miss the surprise look on your face? No way. It was priceless."

Jake pulled Brianna's chair back, and she took her seat. "I should have known you were near. I thought I saw you earlier today near the aquarium. Why didn't you make yourself known?"

"I didn't know you were near," he lied.

Brianna's stomach growled. "Hold that thought. I need some food."

"So what did you do today?"

Brianna described some of her tour excursions. She didn't mean to get animated but couldn't help it, because it was the first time she had swam with dolphins.

"I should have come a day earlier. I would have loved to have seen you."

"I have pictures."

"But there's nothing like experiencing it for yourself."

Dinner with Jake seemed natural. They laughed. They talked. Things didn't seem tense, like they did back in Dallas. After going back and forth on who would pay for the meal, Brianna relented and let him pay. Besides, in a few short weeks, she would be back to paying for everything.

Jake convinced her to join him in the casino. The vibe in the casino made her want to play the slot machines. Jake headed straight for the blackjack tables, so she followed suit. After winning the first few hands, he started losing.

"Do you want to play?" he asked.

"I'm not good at it."

"Come on. Play a few hands." He handed her some chips. "Use these."

"Don't get mad if I lose them now."

"Have some fun." He moved out of the seat and let her sit down.

Brianna had to admit, playing blackjack was fun, especially since she didn't have to worry about losing any of her money. She won and lost a few hands, but by the time she finished, she was ahead by 250 dollars. She handed the chips to Jake. "I think these belong to you."

"They're yours."

"In that case, let's go cash them in so we can play the slots."

Brianna had fun playing the slots. When she hit the jackpot, she didn't know who was more excited, her or Jake. The coins from the machine overflowed onto the floor. One of the casino workers helped them put them in a huge tray. She jumped up and down. Jake wrapped his arm around her waist as the casino cashier counted out the coins. Brianna opted to have the money wired to her bank account. She didn't want anyone to hit her upside the head and take her money before she had time to enjoy it.

"Looks like you can afford to treat me to a night out on the town," Jake joked.

She looped her arm through Jake's. "Can you believe it? Two hundred thousand dollars. From a slot machine. I've been to Shreveport and played the slots, and the most I ever won was maybe a hundred dollars."

"Try the blackjack tables the next time."

"Only if you come with me," she said, flirting.

"How about a nightcap?"

"It's been a long day. Besides, I'm sure you're tired."

"What's on your agenda for tomorrow?"

"I'm going to the Straw Market."

The elevator door opened. Brianna pressed seven. She waited for Jake to press his floor, but he never did.

He asked, "Do you mind if I tag along?"

"It's up to you. I plan on being there all day."

"I'll sacrifice for you."

"It's a date."

The elevator door opened, and they both exited.

"I'm right down there," Jake informed her.

"So am I."

He extended his hand out. "Lead the way."

CHAPTER 55

Jake's room was right across the hall from Brianna's. Jake waved as she entered her room. She waved back. She let out a huge sigh once she was behind closed doors. Questions ran through her mind. *What is Jake up to? Will he ask me for a divorce now? Couldn't he have waited until I got back to the States?* To unwind, Brianna lounged on her balcony and enjoyed the ocean breeze. On this moonlit night, she had a beautiful view of the ocean and sand. The knock at the door broke the trance. She looked through the peephole.

"What's up?" Brianna asked when she opened the door and found Jake standing there in his blue terry-cloth robe.

"You," he said as he walked across the threshold and kissed her with an intensity that left her breathless.

Jake swooped her up in his arms and carried her to the bed. Brianna wanted to resist, but her body didn't agree with her mind. "Jake, maybe we should wait," she said, not wanting him to stop.

"I've waited months. I want you, Bri, and I can't wait another day."

"But . . . ," she said as his lips enclosed her right nipple. Her body arched, and the only sounds out of her mouth at this point were moans.

"I want you, Bri. Tell me that you want me, too."

"Jake," she said between clenched teeth as his kisses found her G-spot.

"I love you, Brianna," he said as he looked into her eyes and their bodies united.

"I love you, too, Jake."

The moment she said those words, Jake seemed to swell within her. They couldn't seem to get enough of each other. Multiple orgasms erupted through her, sending her body into a spasm. She called out his name. He called out her name. Their souls united. No one else mattered but Jake. Pleasing Jake.

They made love throughout the night and off and on the next day. The sun beaming through the opened balcony door woke Brianna up. Jake wrapped his arms around her body. She snuggled closer to him. She closed her eyes. She fell back asleep and woke when she felt Jake move.

"What time is it?" Jake asked as he squeezed her.

"I have no idea."

Jake moved so he could see the clock. "Dear, we've been asleep all day. It's almost six o'clock."

"I didn't realize it was that late."

"Neither did I. Let's go out tonight. I'll go get dressed and meet you back here in, say, an hour."

Jake didn't wait for her to respond. He got up and wrapped his robe around his body. He looked so sexy that her body longed for him to return to her bed. She knew if she called out his name, he would be happy to oblige; instead, she remained quiet and watched him walk out the door.

Jake's phone rang as he was putting on his shoes. "Mr. Banks, everything's ready," the hotel manager said on the other end.

"Thank you. We'll be down in a few minutes."

Brianna had come into Jake's life like a whirlwind, and he couldn't imagine his life without her. It had taken half a lifetime to find someone who he genuinely cared for. Many women had tried to make him love them, but they had failed. Brianna hadn't tried, yet she had his heart. If they had to stay on Paradise Island for the rest of their lives, he would sell his company and do so. There was no way he would let Brianna divorce him.

He went across the hall to get Brianna. Wearing a strapless, short, black sequined dress and four-inch crystal-clear Cinderella heels, she had him mesmerized. He wanted to take his jacket off and cover her up so no other man could look at her. Jake knew what kind of thoughts would cross men's minds, because he was having quite a few naughty ones himself. He brushed the curls flowing from the sides of Brianna's pent-up hair and kissed her on the cheek.

"I hope I didn't overdress."

Jake wanted to respond, "Undress." But instead he said, "You look great, as usual."

They rode in the black stretch limousine to the pier. Jake helped Brianna get on the rented yacht. "Welcome to the *Enchanted*," the captain said. "My staff is here to serve. Madame, can we get you a drink?"

"I'll have a Sprite for now," Brianna responded.

"And you, sir?"

"Nothing for me right now," replied Jake.

They followed the captain into what appeared to be a dining room. The tables were covered in fine china.

"I'll send a waitress in to take your order. I've included a menu on the table," the captain informed them. He then pulled Brianna's chair out.

When they were left alone, Brianna said, "I could get used to this service."

"Stick with me, kid," Jake said as he winked his right eye.

They were served a six-course meal. After dessert, Brianna pushed her chair away from the table and said, "I can't eat another bite."

Jake extended his hand out to Brianna. She placed hers on top of his. He escorted her to the stairway that led to the deck. They walked hand in hand around the yacht. They were miles away from the pier. The light from the full moon gleamed on the ocean waves. The sounds of the ocean could be hypnotizing.

There would never be a more perfect time to bring up the subject of their anniversary to Brianna. She seemed relaxed. He felt relaxed. "Bri, look at me."

She turned to face him. "I had planned on giving you this long speech, but words escape me now. All I know is, Bri . . . . Brianna, I don't want you to leave me. Our anniversary is coming up, and I don't want a divorce. Give me another year to prove to you that we can make this work."

She placed the palm of her hand on his cheek. Her gentle gesture surprised him. "Jake, do you really think we can? It started off all wrong. I don't know. Maybe this time here is all we have. Let's not ruin it."

He touched her hand. "I know we can have more. I love you. You confessed to still loving me last night."

She turned away. "Love isn't enough. Your company is doing better than ever. You don't need me. I've served my purpose. Besides, you don't know the whole story."

"I know all I need to know."

"Jake, I accepted your original proposal because of what your uncle did to my father. So, see, we both had ulterior motives for getting hitched."

"I don't care about that. We can start over."

"It's too late for us."

"What do you want me to do? Beg? Beg? Is that it?" He got down on one knee. "If that's what it takes, I will. I beg you. Please don't leave me. I love you, and I know we didn't start off the traditional way, but we can make our marriage work."

Brianna reached for him. "Get up. That look is not becoming," she teased.

"So is that a yes, Jake?"

"It's an I'll think about it."

"That's all I can ask for." They kissed as the moonlight beamed down on them.

They spent the night on the yacht, making love in a private cabin. Jake made a mental note to tip the captain and the hotel manager for providing the background to another perfect night in the Bahamas.

Brianna lay in his arms. She looked like Sleeping Beauty waiting on her prince. He would be her prince, her king, her everything if she would allow him to be. He hoped the time on the island would be enough to make her see that the two of them belonged together.

If Jake could bottle up this euphoric feeling of love, he would. The stores wouldn't be able to keep the bottles on the shelves. Love could be a good thing when it was reciprocated, but when it wasn't, it hurt like hell. He hoped he would no longer have to be the recipient of the cruelty that love could offer. The past few months of living under the same roof with Brianna without being able to fully express himself had frustrated him more times than he cared to admit. Jake hoped this trip was the beginning, and not the prelude to the end, of their relationship.

CHAPTER 56

Brianna couldn't believe how wonderful the trip to the Bahamas had ended up being. She didn't want to return to Dallas. Now here she was, in her room across from Jake's, waiting to see if he would come home from work early and hoping he would. They had been back only a day, but she missed him already.

Brianna couldn't concentrate on her business. Her mind, consumed with her trip to the Bahamas, replayed their last night together. Jake had begged for her to give their relationship another try. It would be so easy to give in to her feelings for him. She would make a decision by night's end.

Tired of waiting on Jake to come home, she grabbed the gifts she had brought back from her trip and decided to make a few stops. Bradford met her over at Bridget and Matt's.

"Sis, you know how to pick out some good gifts. Next time bring me a Bahama mama, though," Bradford joked.

Bridget said, "All these women over here, and you want to mess up the women over there, too."

"Stop it now," Brianna shouted. "Dani's only three months old, and she acts better than you two."

"I love my present," Bradford said as he got up and hugged her.

Brianna playfully pushed him away. "Get away."

Matt walked in with Danielle. "There's my favorite niece," Brianna said.

"Your only niece, I hope," Bridget commented.

"I wrap mine up," Bradford said.

"TMI, bro," Brianna said as she took her niece from Matt and held her. "Auntie got you something, too." She used her free hand and retrieved a beautiful blue chiffon dress from her shopping bag. "Isn't this the cutest little dress?"

"You're spoiling her," Bridget said.

"That's what aunts are for," Brianna reminded her.

"Toys, clothes. Where are we going to put all this stuff?" Matt complained.

"Don't worry, Matt. In about another month or so, you'll be able to get a bigger house or expand this one," quipped Bradford.

Brianna felt a wet spot on her pant legs. "Seems like somebody needs their diaper changed."

"I got her," Matt said.

"I'm going to let you get her, too, because I think she passed gas." Brianna handed Danielle to Matt. After Matt was out of the room, Brianna said, "I know you two are probably wondering about me and Jake."

Bradford said, "Forget you and Jake. I want to know when I'm getting my one mill."

Bridget took a pillow off the sofa and hit him

with it. "Shut up, doofus . . . When will the divorce be final?"

"That's just it. There's not going to be a divorce," Brianna confessed.

Bridget said, "What? Before your trip, that's all you talked about."

"My emotions have been on a roller-coaster ride for a while now. But I'm tired of fighting it. I'm going to give our marriage a real try."

Bridget wrapped her arms around her. "If he makes you happy, then you have my support."

Bradford asked, "What about the money?"

"We're still getting it. Staying with Jake doesn't interfere with it. My attorney has made sure of it," Brianna explained.

"Sis, it's your life. Live it," Bradford said.

"I'm tired of hurting. I forgave him. Dad is no longer here, and me holding on to the anger I had isn't going to bring him back," Brianna explained.

"You know, the more I think about it, it was kind of silly for us to be holding Jake accountable for something that his uncle did, anyway," Bradford said.

"True. But it sure felt good blaming someone," Bridget added. "But Brad's right. It's time to let it go."

They hugged each other. Matt returned, holding Danielle. "Once again, I feel left out."

CHAPTER 57

Jake looked forward to making it home after a long day at work but was disappointed when Brianna wasn't there. He called her on her cell phone but got her voice mail. He checked her bedroom and was relieved to see her things there. Until she answered his question about whether or not she was divorcing him, he would not relax completely.

"Jake, I'm home," Brianna yelled from downstairs.

"I'm up here," he responded.

"I dropped off the gifts. Danielle loved hers. She drooled all over her doll. Christopher was asking for his daddy."

"Aw. You should have waited for me. I would have loved to have seen the two of them."

"You'll have plenty of time. Nikki is dropping Christopher off this weekend. She and Byron have a party to go to."

Jake didn't let her finish before kissing her. "You were saying?" he asked as he moved from in front of the stairway to let her pass by.

Brianna licked her lips. "I don't know. My mind . . . It went blank."

They laughed. "It was kind of lonely in my bed last night," Jake said as he followed her to her room.

"You don't say." She opened her door. "We'll have to change that." Without saying another word, she went inside the room and shut the door.

He went back downstairs to do a few things in his office. His private line rang. "Are you coming upstairs, or do I have to come down and get you?" Brianna asked.

"I'll be there before you hang up," Jake said, feeling as horny as a teenaged boy. He didn't bother to turn off his laptop. He saw the flicker of light from the candle before reaching the bedroom doorway. A floral scent filled the air. Brianna sat on top of the covers, looking like a playboy bunny with her see-through, white chiffon lingerie trimmed with white, fluffy sleeves. She got on her knees in the bed and reached for him.

Jake allowed Brianna to take full control. Minutes later, she was straddling him and driving him out of his mind. She was making up for lost time, and he was glad to be the recipient. He felt like silly putty in her hands as she brought him to the brink many times that night.

The next morning marked their anniversary. Jake treated Brianna to breakfast in bed.

Brianna, with a huge grin on her face, said, "Dear, you didn't have to do this. Aren't you going to be late for work?"

"I'm taking the day off. Today's our day," he responded.

There were several people coming by his house to set up his surprise gift for Brianna. He had a full day planned for them outside the house. They spent the day at an exclusive downtown spa. They were floating when they returned home.

"I'm thirsty. I'll be upstairs in a minute," Brianna said.

"What do you want to drink? Remember, today's your day, and I'm serving you," Jake said, not once letting his arm leave her shoulders.

"Just a glass of ice-cold water."

"I got it. I'll meet you upstairs. Check your room. There's a dress I want you to put on for me tonight."

"Jake, you're spoiling me," she responded.

"That's my intention."

Jake walked through the formal dining room. The tables were decorated with purple and violet flowers, as instructed. Betty had located matching china. The guests would soon be arriving. He took Brianna her glass of water.

"This dress is beautiful," she said as she twirled with it in front of her.

"I'm going to get dressed. I'll come get you when I'm ready," Jake said, handing Brianna the water.

An hour later, Jake knocked on Brianna's door. She didn't answer at first, so he was afraid his little surprise was spoiled. He was turning to head down the stairs when she opened her door and called out his name.

"Baby, you look gorgeous."

"So do you," Brianna responded. She adjusted his tie.

A young man dressed in a black tuxedo walked up the stairway. "Dinner is ready, sir."

Brianna looked at him. "Wow. Full service tonight."

He winked. He led her down the stairs. The same young man who had met them on the stairway opened the door to the formal dining room. Brianna's family and friends and Jake's family and friends were seated at the table. They all stood up as the couple entered.

"Jake, you didn't tell me we were having company," cried Brianna.

"I wanted it to be a surprise," he told her.

"It is. I thought . . . Never mind," she responded. "Thanks."

CHAPTER 58

Brianna had to admit that after a day of pampering, she hadn't expected a party in honor of their one-year anniversary. He had gone out of his way to be a loving husband since they'd returned from the Bahamas. She greeted her guests. "Why didn't you tell me about this?" she whispered in Bridget's ear when she hugged her.

"Your husband asked us not to," Bradford responded for her.

"Traitors," Brianna joked. "Tosha, thanks for coming."

"I wouldn't have missed this for anything in the world," Tosha whispered. "I see you two worked things out."

"I'll talk to you about it later," Brianna told her.

Everyone took their seats. Jake stood up. "Thank you all for coming. I wanted to invite some of our close friends and family here tonight to help us celebrate our one-year anniversary."

Cheers were heard around the room.

Jake went on. "Bri can tell you that we've had some challenges. However, I can stand here today and say we made it, and we look forward to year two." Jake looked at Brianna. "Brianna, I think I'm happier today than I was on our wedding day. I love you more than I thought possible. I pray you'll remain by my side until death do us part."

Brianna wiped the tears forming in the corners of her eyes. She stood up and kissed him.

Trent cleared his throat. "Get a room."

People laughed.

"Since I'm standing," Brianna said, "I have a few things I want to say." She noticed Bridget squirm. "It'll only take a minute. I know you're all hungry." She looked at Jake. "Jake used to tease me about being his invisible wife, because we were on two different schedules." She paused. "I resigned from Banks Telecom because I felt the need to branch out on my own."

Jake reached for her hand. She squeezed his, then went on. "Jake could have tried to persuade me to stay, but he didn't. He's not one of those men who feels like he has to control his woman. I appreciate that. Jake, I stand before you, our family, and friends to say that I love you. I plan on being by your side forever, and there's nothing you can do about it." She looked around the room.

She heard Jake sigh. She kissed him again.

Cheers were heard throughout the room. Jake said, "Okay, let's eat."

Brianna and Jake couldn't take their eyes off each other. After dinner, they were led to the back of the house, where there was a live band playing. "Drink and be merry," Jake announced. He turned to face Brianna. "I have another surprise, but I'll wait until everyone leaves."

Brianna tilted her head to the side. "Can I get it now? Please."

"Close your eyes." He turned to Bridget. "Make sure she keeps her eyes closed."

A few minutes later, he returned with a big box. Tosha seemed more excited about the gift than Brianna did. "Open it," Tosha said.

Several people surrounded her as she lifted the top off the box. A Yorkshire terrier peeped her head out. "Aw, she's adorable," Brianna said as the puppy climbed its way out of the box.

"Happy anniversary, baby," Jake said.

Brianna kissed him, and the puppy jumped in between the two of them.

"Hey, I might have to take you back if you're going to be blocking my action," said Jake.

"What's her name?" Brianna asked.

"It's up to you, dear."

"Lovie, because she's so adorable."

Brianna opened up the rest of her anniversary gifts, but none were more special than Lovie. She was sure other folks would think Jake was being cheap, but this was one of the most romantic gifts he could have gotten her, especially since she knew how much he hated dogs.

She was playing with Lovie in the living room when Jake came into the room. "Everybody's gone. It's just you and me." The doorbell rang. "I guess someone forgot something."

"Overton, what are you doing here?" she heard Jake say. She, too, was wondering why his lawyer was showing up at this time of night on their anniversary.

"I wanted to hand deliver this to you myself. It's a note from your uncle."

Jake looked at the envelope. "It's addressed to Brianna."

Brianna walked to where they stood and took the envelope away from Jake.

"Maybe you should sit down," Overton suggested.

They all went back to the living room. Lovie barked. She was already protective of her owner. Brianna petted her with one hand while reading the letter. "It says, he's happy that I made his nephew happy. He calls you his son several times in the letter. He also apologizes for what happened with my father. I don't understand."

"Keep reading," Overton said.

Brianna's mouth flew open. "Wow. He was in love with my mother at one time. I can't believe it."

Jake said, "He said the same thing in the letter I got."

Brianna blinked. "You mean you knew about this and didn't tell me?"

"I was going to tell you, but we were having issues then, and then we resolved them. To be honest, Uncle Jack and his issues were the last thing on my mind."

Brianna didn't know what to think. Life with Jake seemed to be filled with drama. Just when they got over one hurdle, it seemed something else hit them. "This is a lot to digest. Can you take care of Lovie? I think I need to lie down." She stood up. "Overton, thanks for this. Things are so much clearer."

She made a three-way call to her sister and brother and read the letter to them. They were both in awe.

Bridget said, "I should have known something was behind him putting you as a stipulation in that will."

"I'm tripping off the part about him being in love with Mom," Bradford said.

"He held a grudge a long time," Brianna said.

Bradford said, "I just wished his conscience would have set in before Dad died."

"We got closure," Bridget said.

Brianna hung up with her siblings. Her thoughts went back to Jake. She had made several mistakes since knowing him. Jake had forgiven her and wanted to work on their relationship. She had no choice. Brianna had to follow her heart. She decided to forgive Jake for not telling her about the contents of Jack's letter.

Brianna watched Jake play with Lovie from the living-room doorway. She walked behind him and wrapped her arms around his shoulders and said, "I meant what I said earlier. I don't plan on going anywhere. I love you, and there's nothing you can do about it."

"Good, because I would really hate to fight for custody of little Lovie," he teased.

She hit him on his arm. "Oh, you got jokes."

Jake pulled her into his arms, and they both fell back on the couch. "As long as I can keep seeing those cute dimples of yours, I have plenty of them."

"Jake, promise me one thing."

"What's that, sweetheart?"

"Going forward you won't keep any secrets from me."

"Promise. And the same goes for you," Jake said.

Brianna responded, "It's a deal."

"I love you, Bri. Thanks for giving us another try."

They sealed their deal with a kiss.

His Invisible Wife
Reading Group Guide

1. Was Brianna wrong for blaming Jake for what happened to her father?

2. How do you feel about Jake approaching Brianna with his proposition?

3. Would you have accepted or turned him down? Why or why not?

4. What do you think about Trent? Tosha? Bridget? Bradford?

5. Did you think Brianna would go through with the setup with her friend Lisa?

6. What is your opinion of Jake?

7. What did you think about the way Brianna reacted to/handled the women from Jake's past?

8. Why do you think it was hard for Brianna and Jake to admit they loved one another?

9. How much money would it take for you to leave your boyfriend or spouse?

10. Trent thought Uncle Jack was a little eccentric. Do you agree?

11. How long do you hold on to grudges?

12. If you read *My Invisible Husband,* were you surprised to see Byron and Nikki Matthews make an appearance in *His Invisible Wife*?

13. Do you think the judge was being fair when she gave them joint custody of Christopher?

14. What do you think of Brianna's acceptance of Jake's child? Would you have supported his efforts?

ABOUT THE AUTHOR

Shelia M. Goss is the nationally best-selling author of *My Invisible Husband; Roses Are Thorns, Violets Are True; Paige's Web;* and *Double Platinum.* She pursues unique storylines: her motto is "bringing you stories with a twist." She is the recipient of three Shades of Romance Magazine Readers' Choice Multi-Cultural Awards and was honored by inclusion in *Literary Divas: The Top 100+ Most Admired African-American Women in Literature.*

Besides writing fiction, she is an entertainment writer. She's interviewed such celebrities as Mary J. Blige, Michael Bolton, Vivica Fox, Star Jones, and Brian McKnight. Her articles have appeared in national magazines, such as *Black Romance, Caribbean Posh,* and *Jolie.* Shelia would love to hear from you. Her e-mail address is sheliagoss@aol.com, or visit her Web site at http://www.sheliagoss.com or www.myspace.com/sheliagoss.